This special signed
edition is limited to
500 numbered copies
and
26 lettered copies.

This is copy

_111_ .

The Kragen

The Kragen

Jack Vance

SUBTERRANEAN PRESS 2007

First Edition

ISBN
978-1-59606-151-4

Subterranean Press
PO Box 190106
Burton, MI 48519

www.subterraneanpress.com

CHAPTER i

AMONG THE PEOPLE of the Floats caste distinctions were fast losing their old-time importance. The Anarchists and Procurers had disappeared altogether; intercaste marriages were by no means uncommon, especially when they involved castes of approximately the same social status. Society of course was not falling into chaos; the Bezzlers and the Incendiaries still maintained their traditional aloofness; the Advertisermen still could not evade a subtle but nonetheless general disesteem, and where the castes were associated with a craft or trade, they functioned with undiminished effectiveness. The Swindlers comprised the vast majority of those who fished from coracles; Blackguards constructed all the sponge-arbors in every lagoon; the Hoodwinks completely monopolized the field of hood-winking. This last relationship always excited the curiosity of the young, who would inquire, "Which first:

the Hoodwinks or hood-winking?" To which the elders customarily replied, "When the Ship of Space discharged our ancestors upon these blessed floats, there were four Hoodwinks among the Eighty-Three. Later, when the towers were built and the lamps established, there were hoods to wink, and it seemed nothing less than apposite that the Hoodwinks should occupy themselves at the trade. It may well be that matters stood so in the Outer Wildness, before the Escape. It seems likely. There were undoubtedly lamps to be flashed and hoods to be winked. Of course there is much we do not know, much concerning which the Dicta are silent."

Whether or not the Hoodwinks had been drawn to the trade by virtue of ancient use, it was now the rare Hoodwink who did not in some measure find his vocation upon the towers, either as a rigger, a lamp-tender, or as full-fledged hoodwink.

Another caste, the Larceners, constructed the towers, which customarily stood sixty to ninety feet high at the center of the float, directly above the primary stalk of the sea-plant; there were usually four legs of woven withe, which passed through holes in the pad to join a stout stalk twenty or thirty feet below the surface. At the top of the tower was a cupola, with walls of split withe, a roof of gummed and laminated pad-skin. Yard-arms extending to either side supported lattices, each carrying nine lamps arranged in a square, three to the side, together with the hoods and trip-mechanisms. Within the cupola, windows afforded a view across the water to the neighboring floats—as much as two miles or as little as a quarter-mile distant. The Master Hoodwink sat at a panel. At his left hand were nine tap-rods, cross-coupled to lamp-hoods on the lattice to his right. Similarly the tap-rods at his right hand controlled the hoods to his left. By this means the configurations he formed and those he received, from his point of view, were of identical aspect and caused him no confusion. During the daytime, the lamps were not lit and white targets served the same function. The hoodwink set his configuration with quick strokes of right and left hands, kicked the release, which thereupon flicked the hoods or shutters at the respective lamps or targets. Each configuration signified a word; the mastery of a lexicon and a sometimes remarkable dexterity were the Master Hoodwink's stock in trade. All could send at speeds approximating that of speech; all knew at least four thousand, and some six, seven or even nine thousand configurations. The folk of the floats could in varying degrees read the configurations, which were also employed in the keeping of the archives, and other communications, memoranda and messages.*

On Tranque Float, at the extreme east of the group, the Master Hoodwink was one Chaezy Zander, a rigorous and ex-

---

* The orthography had been adopted in the earliest days and was highly systematic. The cluster at the left indicated the genus of the idea, the cluster at the right denoted the specific. In such a fashion ⠿ at the left, signified color, and hence:

White	⠿	•
Black	⠿	•
Red	⠿	• •
Pink	⠿	• •
Dark Red	⠿	• • •

and so forth.

acting old man with a mastery of over eight thousand configurations. His first assistant, Sklar Hast, had well over five thousand configurations at his disposal. There were two further assistants, as well as three apprentices, two riggers, a lamp-tender and a maintenance withe-weaver, this latter a Larcener. Chaezy Zander tended the tower from dusk until middle evening: the busy hours during which gossip, announcements, news and notifications regarding King Kragen flickered up and down the fifty-mile line of the floats.

Sklar Hast winked hoods during the afternoon; then, when Chaezy Zander appeared in the cupola, he looked to maintenance and supervised the apprentices. A relatively young man, Sklar Hast had achieved his status by working in accordance with a simple and uncomplicated policy: without compromise and with great tenacity he strove for excellence, and sought to instill the same standards into the apprentices. He was an almost brutally direct man, without affability, knowing nothing of either malice, guile, tact or patience. The apprentices disliked but respected him; Chaezy Zander considered him over-pragmatic and deficient in reverence for his betters, notably himself. Sklar Hast cared nothing one way or the other. Chaezy Zander must soon retire; in due course Sklar Hast would become Master Hoodwink. He was in no hurry; on this placid, limpid, changeless world, time drifted rather than throbbed. In the meantime, life was easy and for the most part pleasant. Sklar Hast owned a small pad of which he was the sole occupant. The pad, a leaf of spongy tissue a hundred feet in diameter braced by tough woody radial ribs, floated in the lagoon, separated from the main float by twenty feet of water.

Sklar Hast's hut was of standard construction: sea-plant withe bent and lashed, then sheathed with sheets of pad-skin, the tough near-transparent membrane peeled from the bottom of the sea-plant pad. All was then coated with well-aged varnish, prepared by boiling sea-plant sap until the water was driven off and the resins amalgamated.

On the pad grew other vegetation: shrubs rooted in the spongy tissue, a thicket of bamboo-like rods yielding a good-quality withe, epiphytes hanging from the central spike of the sea-plant—this rising twenty or thirty feet to terminate in a coarse white spore-producing organ. Most of the plants of the pad yielded produce of benefit to man: fruit, fiber, dye, drug or decorative foliage. On other pads the plants might be ordered according to aesthetic theory; Sklar Hast had small taste in these matters, and the center of his pad was little more than an untidy copse of various stalks, fronds, tendrils and leaves, in various shades of black, green and rusty orange.

Sklar Hast reckoned himself a lucky man. As a Hoodwink by caste and Assistant Master Hoodwink by trade he enjoyed a not inconsiderable prestige. Standing before his hut, Sklar Hast watched the gold and lavender dusk and its dark pastel reflection in the ocean. The afternoon rain had freshened and cooled the air; now the evening breeze arose to rustle the foliage and brush susurrations across the water...Chaezy Zander was growing old. Sklar Hast wondered how long the old man would persist in fulfilling the rigorous exactitude of his duties. True, he showed no lapse whatever in precision or flexibility of usage, but almost insensibly his speed was falling off. Sklar Hast could out-wink him without difficulty should he choose to do so; a capability which Sklar Hast, for all his bluntness, had so far not demonstrated. Useless folly to irritate the old man! Sklar Hast suspected that even now he delayed his retirement mainly out of jealousy and antipathy toward Sklar Hast.

There was no hurry. Life seemed to extend ahead of him as wide and lucid as the dreaming expanse of water and sky which filled his vision. On this water-world, which had no name, there were no seasons, no tides, no storms, no change, very little anxiety regarding time. Sklar Hast was currently testing five or six girls of orthodox Hoodwink background for marital suitability. In due course, he would make a choice, and enlarge his hut. And forever abandon privacy, Sklar Hast reflected wistfully. There was definitely no need for haste. He would continue to test such girls as were eligible, and perhaps a few others as well. Meanwhile, life was good. In the lagoon hung arbors on which grew the succulent sponge-like organisms which when cleaned, plucked and boiled, formed the staple food of the Float-folk. The lagoon teemed likewise with other edible fish, separated from the predators of the ocean by the enormous net which hung in a great hemisphere from various buoys, pads and the main float—this a complex of ancient pads, compressed, wadded and interlocked to create an unbroken surface five acres in area and varying from two feet to six feet in thickness. There was much other food available: spores from the sea-plant fruiting organ, from which a crusty bread could be baked. There were in addition other flowers, tendrils and bulbs, as well as the prized flesh of the gray-fish to take which the Swindlers must fare forth in their coracles and cunningly swindle from the ocean, which horizon to horizon, pole to pole, enveloped the entire surface of the world.

Sklar Hast turned his eyes up to the skies, where the constellations already blazed with magnificent ardor. To the south, half-up the sky, hung a cluster of twenty-five middle-bright stars, from which, so tradition asserted, his ancestors had fled in the Ship of Space, finally to reach the world of water. Eighty-three persons, of various castes, managed to disembark before the ship foundered and sank; the eighty-three had become twenty thousand, scattered east and west along fifty miles of floating sea-plant. The castes, so jealously differentiated during the first few generations, with the Bezzlers at the top and the Advertisermen at the bottom, had now accommodated themselves to one another and were even intermingling. There was little to disturb the easy flow of life; nothing harsh nor unpleasant—except, perhaps, King Kragen.

Sklar Hast made a sour face and examined those three of his arbors which only two days before had been plucked clean by King Kragen, whose appetite as well as his bulk grew by the year. Sklar Hast scowled westward across the ocean, in the direction from which King Kragen customarily appeared, moving with long strokes of his four propulsive vanes, in a manner to suggest some vast, distorted, grotesquely ugly anthropoid form swimming by means of the breaststroke. There, of course, the resemblance to man ended. King Kragen's body was tough black cartilage, a cylinder on a rectangle, from the corners of which extended the vanes. The cylinder comprising King Kragen's main bulk opened forward in a maw fringed with four mandibles and eight palps, and aft in an anus. Atop this cylinder, somewhat to the front, rose a turret from which the four eyes protruded: two peering forward, two aft. During Sklar Hast's lifetime King Kragen had grown perceptibly, and now measured perhaps sixty feet in length. King Kragen was a terrible force for destruction, but luckily could be placated. King Kragen enjoyed copious quantities of sponges and when his appetite was appeased he injured no one and did no damage; indeed he kept the area clear of other marauding kragen, which either he killed or sent flapping and skipping in a panic across the ocean.

Sklar Hast's attention was attracted by a dark swirl in the water at the edge of the net: a black bulk surrounded by glistening cusps and festoons of starlit water. Sklar Hast ran forward to the edge of the pad, peered. No question about it! A lesser kragen was attempting to break the net that it might plunder the lagoon!

Sklar Hast shouted a curse, shook his fist, turned, ran at full speed across the pad. He jumped into his coracle, crossed the twenty feet of water to the central float. He delayed only long enough to tie the coracle to a stake formed of a human femur, then ran at top speed to the hoodwink tower.

A mile to the west the tower on Thrasneck Float flickered its lamps, the configurations coming with the characteristic style of Durdan Farr, the Thrasneck Master Hoodwink: *"...thirteen...bushels...of...salt...lost...when...a...barge...took...water...between...Sumber...and...Adelvine..."*

Sklar Hast climbed the ladder, burst into the cupola. He pointed to the lagoon. "A rogue, breaking the nets. I just saw him. Call King Kragen!"

Chaezy Zander instantly flashed the cut-in signal. His fingers jammed down rods, he kicked the release. *"Call…King… Kragen!"* he signaled. *"Rogue…in…Tranque…Lagoon!"*

On Thrasneck Float Durdan Farr relayed the message to the tower on Bickle Float, and so along the line of floats to Sciona at the far west, who thereupon returned the signal: *"King…Kragen…is…nowhere…at…hand."*

Back down the line of towers flickered the message, returning to Tranque Float in something short of sixty seconds. Sklar Hast read the message as it left the Bickle Tower, before reaching Thrasneck, and rushed over to the side of the cupola, to peer down into the lagoon.

Others had now discovered the rogue kragen and set up a shout to the tower, "Call King Kragen!" Sklar Hast shouted in return, "He can't be found!" Chaezy Zander, tight-lipped, was already dispatching another message: *"To…the…various… intercessors…along…the…line. Kindly…summon…King…Kragen…and…direct…him…to…Tranque…Float.*

Sklar Hast pointed and bellowed, "Look! The beast has broken the net! Where is Voidenvo?"

He swung down the ladder, ran to the edge of the lagoon. The kragen, a beast perhaps fifteen feet in length, was surging easily through the water, a caricature of a man performing the breast-stroke. Starlight danced and darted along the disturbed water, and so outlined the gliding black bulk. Sklar Hast cried out in fury: the brute was headed for his arbors, so recently devastated by the appetite of King Kragen! It could not be borne! He ran to his coracle, returned to his pad. Already the kragen had extended its palps and was feeling for sponges.

Sklar Hast sought for an implement which might serve as a weapon; there was nothing to hand: a few articles fashioned from human bones and fish cartilage. Leaning against the hut was a boat-hook, a stalk ten feet long, carefully straightened, scraped, and seasoned, to which a hook-shaped human rib had been lashed. He took it up and now from the central pad came a cry of remonstrance. "Sklar Hast! What do you do?" This was the voice of Semon Voidenvo the Intercessor. Sklar Hast paid him no heed. He ran to the edge of the pad, jabbed the boat-hook at the kragen's turret. It scraped uselessly along resilient cartilage. The kragen swung up one of its vanes, knocked the pole aside. Sklar Hast jabbed the pole with all his strength at what he considered the kragen's most vulnerable area: a soft pad of receptor-endings directly above the maw. Behind him he heard Semon Voidenvo's outraged protest: "This is not to be done! This is not to be done! Desist!"

The kragen quivered at the blow, twisted its massive turret to gaze at Sklar Hast. Again it swung up its fore-vane, smashing the pole, slashing at Sklar Hast, who leapt back with inches to spare. From the central pad Semon Voidenvo bawled, "By no means molest the kragen; it is a matter for the King! We must respect the King's perquisites!"

Sklar Hast stood back in fury as the kragen resumed its feeding. As if to punish Sklar Hast for his assault, it passed close beside the arbors, worked its vanes, and the arbors, sea-plant stalk lashed with fiber, collapsed. Sklar Hast groaned. "No more than you deserve," called out Semon Voidenvo with odious complacence. "You interfered with the duties of King Kragen, now your arbors are destroyed. This is justice."

"'Justice'? Bah!" bellowed Sklar Hast. "Where is King Kragen? You, Voidenvo the Intercessor! Why don't you summon the great gluttonous beast?"

"Come, come," admonished Semon Voidenvo. "This is not the tone in which to speak of King Kragen."

Sklar Hast thrust himself and his coracle back to the central float, where now stood several hundred folk of Tranque Float. He pointed. "Look. See that vile beast of the sea. He is plundering us of our goods. I say, kill him. I say that we need not suffer such molestation."

Semon Voidenvo emitted a high-pitched croak. "Are you insane? Someone, pour water on this maniac hoodwink, who has too long focused his eyes on flashing lights."

In the lagoon the kragen moved to the arbors of the Belrod family, deep-divers for stalk and withe, of the Advertiserman caste and prone to a rude and surly vulgarity. The Belrod elder, Poe, a squat large-featured man, still resilient and vehement despite his years, emitted a series of hoots, intended to distract the kragen, which instead tore voraciously at the choicest Belrod sponges.

"I say, kill the beast!" cried Sklar Hast. "The King despoils us, must we likewise feed all the kragen of the ocean?"

"Kill the beast!" echoed the younger Belrods.

Semon Voidenvo gesticulated in vast excitement, but Poe Belrod shoved him roughly aside. "Quiet, let us listen to the hoodwink. How would we kill the kragen?"

"Come! I will show you how!"

Thirty or forty men followed him, mostly Swindlers, Advertisemen, Blackguards and Extorters. The remainder hung dubiously back. Sklar Hast led the way to a pile of poles intended for the construction of a storehouse. Each pole, fabricated from withes laid lengthwise and bound in glue, was twenty feet long by eight inches in diameter, and combined great strength with lightness.

Sklar Hast found rope, worked with vicious energy. "Now—lift! Across to my pad!"

Excited by his urgency, the men shouldered the pole, carried it to the lagoon, floated it across to Sklar Hast's pad. Then, crossing in coracles, they dragged the pole up on the pad and carried it across to the edge of the lagoon. At Sklar Hast's direction, they set it down with one end resting on the hard fiber of a rib. "Now," said Sklar Hast. "Now we kill the kragen." He made a noose in the end of a light hawser, advanced toward the kragen, which watched him through the rear-pointing eyes of its turret. Sklar Hast moved slowly, so as not to alarm the creature, which continued to pluck sponges with a contemptuous disregard.

Sklar Hast, crouching, approached the edge of the pad. "Beast!" he called. "Ocean brute! Come closer. Come." He bent, splashed water at the kragen. Provoked, it surged toward him. Sklar Hast waited, and just before it swung its vane, he tossed the noose over its turret. He signaled his men. "Now!" They heaved on the line, dragged the thrashing kragen through the water. Sklar Hast guided the line to the end of the pole. The kragen surged suddenly forward; in the confusion and the dark the men heaving on the rope fell backward. Sklar Hast seized the slack, and dodging a murderous slash of the kragen's forevane he flung a hitch around the end of the pole. He danced back. "Now!" he called. "Pull, pull! Both lines! The beast is as good as dead!"

On each of a pair of lines tied to the head of the pole fifteen men heaved. The pole raised up on its base; the line tautened around the kragen's turret, the men dug in their heels, the base of the pole bit into the hard rib. The pole raised, braced by the angle of the ropes. With majestic deliberation the thrashing kragen was lifted from the water and swung up into the air. From those watching on the central pad came a murmurous moan of fascination and dread.

The kragen made gulping noises, reached its vanes this way and that, to no avail. Sklar Hast surveyed the creature, somewhat at a loss as how to proceed. The project thus far had gone with facility: what next? The men were looking at the kragen in awe, uncomfortable at their own daring, and already were stealing furtive glances out over the ocean. Perfectly calm, it glistened with the reflections of the blazing constellations. Sklar Hast thought to divert their attention. "The nets!" he called out to those on the float. "Where are the Extorters? Repair the nets before we lose all our fish! Are you helpless?"

Certain net-makers, a trade dominated by the Extorter caste, detached themselves from the group, went out in coracles to repair the broken net.

Sklar Hast returned to a consideration of the dangling kragen. At his orders the ropes supporting the tilted pole were made fast to ribs on the surface of the pad; the men now gathered gingerly about the dangling kragen, and speculated as to the best means to kill the creature. Perhaps it was already dead? Someone posed the question; a lad of the Belrods prodded the kragen with a length of stalk and suffered a broken collar-bone from a quick blow of the fore-vane.

Sklar Hast stood somewhat apart, studying the creature. Its hide was tough; its cartilaginous tissue even tougher. He sent one man for a boat-hook, another for a sharp femur-stake, and from the two fashioned a spear.

The kragen hung limp, the vanes swaying, occasionally twitching. Sklar Hast moved forward cautiously, touched the point of the spear to the side of the turret, thrust with all his weight. The point entered the tough hide perhaps half an inch, then broke. The kragen jerked, snorted, a vane slashed out. Sklar Hast sensed the dark flicker of motion, dodged and felt the air move beside his face. The spear-shaft hurtled out over the pond; the vane struck the pole on which the kragen hung, bruising the fibers.

"What a quarrelsome beast!" declared Sklar Hast. "Bring more rope; we must prevent any further such demonstrations."

From the main float came a harsh command: "You are mad-men; why do you risk the displeasure of King Kragen? I decree that you desist from your rash acts!"

This was the voice of Ixon Myrex, the Tranque Arbiter, a Bezzler of great physical power and moral conviction, a man with recognized powers and large prestige. Sklar Hast could not ignore Ixon Myrex as he had Semon Voidenvo. He considered the dangling kragen, looked about at the dubious faces of his comrades. They were hesitating; Ixon Myrex was not a man to be trifled with. Sklar Hast walked truculently to the edge of the pad, peered across the intervening water to the shape of Ixon Myrex.

"The kragen is destroying our arbors, Arbiter Myrex. The King is slothful about his duties, hence—"

Ixon Myrex's voice shook with wrath. "That is no way to speak! You violate the spirit of our relationship with King Kragen!"

Sklar Hast said in a reasonable voice, "King Kragen is nowhere to be seen. The Intercessors who claim such large power run back and forth in futility. We must act for ourselves. Cross the water to my pad. Join us in killing this ravenous beast."

Ixon Myrex held up his hands, which trembled in indignation. "Return the kragen to the lagoon, that thereby—"

"That thereby it may destroy more arbors?" demanded Sklar Hast. "This is not the result I hope for." He took a deep breath and made his decision. "Where is the rope?"

Arbiter Myrex called out in his sternest tones, "You men on the pad! This is how I interpret the customs of Tranque Float: the kragen must be restored to the water, with all haste. No other course is consistent with custom."

Sklar Hast waited. There was an uneasy stirring among the men. He said nothing, but taking up the rope, formed a noose. He crawled forward, flipped up the noose to catch a dangling vane, then crawling back and rising to his feet he circled the creature, binding the dangling vanes. The kragen's motions became increasingly constricted and finally were reduced to spasmodic shudders. Sklar Hast approached the creature from the rear, careful to remain out of reach of mandibles and palps, and made the bonds secure. "Now—the vile beast can only squirm. Lower it to the pad and we will find a means to make its end." The guy ropes were shifted, the pole tilted and swung;

the kragen fell to the surface of the pad, where it lay passive, palps and mandibles moving slightly in and out. It showed no agitation, nor discomfort; perhaps it felt none: the exact degree of the kragen's sensitivity and ratiocinative powers had never been determined.

In the east the sky was lightening where the cluster of flaring blue and white suns known as Phocan's Cauldron began to rise. The ocean glimmered with a leaden sheen, and the folk who stood on the central pad began to glance furtively along the obscure horizon, muttering and complaining. Some few called out encouragement to Sklar Hast, recommending the most violent measures against the kragen. Between these and certain others furious arguments raged. Chaezy Zander had descended from the tower, to join Semon Voidenvo and Ixon Myrex, obviously in disapproval of Sklar Hast's activity. Of the Caste Elders only Elmar Pronave, Jackleg and Master Witheweaver, defended Sklar Hast and his unconventional acts.

Sklar Hast ignored all. He sat watching the black hulk with vast distaste, furious with himself for having become involved in so perilous a project. What had been gained? The kragen had broken his arbors; he had revenged himself and prevented more destruction. On the other hand he had incurred the ill-will of the most influential folk of the Float, including Ixon Myrex and Chaezy Zander: no small matter. He likewise had involved those others who had trusted him and looked to him for leadership, and toward whom he now felt responsibility.

He rose to his feet. There was no help for it; the sooner the beast was disposed of, the more quickly life would return to normal. He approached the kragen, examined it gingerly. The mandibles quivered in their anxiety to sever his torso; Sklar Hast stayed warily to the side. How to kill the beast?

Elmar Pronave crossed over from the main float the better to examine the kragen. He was a tall man with a high-bridged broken nose and black hair worn in the two ear-plumes of the old Procurer Caste, now no longer in existence save for a few aggressively unique individuals scattered through the floats, who used the caste-marks to emphasize their emotional detachment.

Pronave circled the hulk, kicked at the rear vane, bent to peer into one of the staring eyes. "If we could cut it up, its parts might be of some use."

"The hide is too tough for our knives," growled Sklar Hast. "There's no neck to be strangled."

"There are other ways to kill."

Sklar Hast nodded. "We could sink the beast into the depths of the ocean—but what to use for weight? Bones? Far too valuable. We could load bags with ash, but there is not that much ash to hand. We could burn every hut on the float as well as the hoodwink tower, and still not secure sufficient. To burn the kragen would require a like mountain of fuel."

A young Larcener who had worked with great enthusiasm during the trapping of the kragen spoke forth: "Poison exists! Find me poison, I will fix a capsule to a stick and push it into the creature's maw!"

Elmar Pronave gave a sardonic bark of laughter. "Agreed; poisons exist, hundreds of them, derived from various sea-plants and animals—but which are sufficiently acrid to destroy this beast? And where is it to be had? I doubt if there is that much poison nearer than Sankeston Float."

Sklar Hast went again to survey the black hulk, and now Phocan's Cauldron, rising into the sky, revealed the kragen in fuller detail. Sklar Hast examined the four blind-seeming eyes in the turret, the intricate construction of the mandibles and tentacles at the maw. He touched the turret, peered at the dome-shaped cap of chitin which covered it. The turret itself seemed laminated, as if constructed of stacked rings of cartilage, the eyes protruding fore and aft in inflexible tubes of a rugose harsh substance. Others in the group began to crowd close; Sklar Hast jumped forward, thrust at a young Felon boat-builder, but too late. The kragen flung out a palp, seized the youth around the neck. Sklar Hast cursed, heaved, tore; the clenched palp was unyielding. Another curled out for his leg; Sklar Hast kicked, danced back, still heaving upon the Felon's writhing form. The kragen drew the Felon slowly forward, hoping, so Sklar Hast realized, to pull him within easier reach. He loosened his grip, but the kragen allowed its palp to sway back to encourage Sklar Hast, who once more tore at the constricting palp. Again the kragen craftily drew its captive and Sklar Hast forward; the second palp snapped out once more and this time coiled around Sklar Hast's leg. Sklar Hast dropped to the ground, twisted himself around and broke the hold, though losing skin. The kragen petulantly jerked the Felon to within reach of its mandible, neatly snipped off the young man's head, tossed body and head aside. A horrified gasp came from the watching crowd. Ixon Myrex bellowed, "Sklar Hast, a man's life is gone, due to your savage obstinacy! You have much to answer for! Woe to you!"

Sklar Hast ignored the imprecation. He ran to his hut, found chisels and a mallet with a head of dense sea-plant stem, brought up from a depth of two hundred feet.* The chisels had blades of pelvic bone ground sharp against a board gritted with the silica husks of foraminifera. Sklar Hast returned to the kragen, put the chisel against the pale lamellum between the chitin dome and the foliations of the turret. He tapped; the chisel penetrated; this, the substance of a new layer being added to the turret, was relatively soft, the consistency of cooked gristle. Sklar Hast struck again; the chisel cut deep. The kragen squirmed.

Sklar Hast worked the chisel back out, made a new incision beside the first, then another and another, working around the periphery of the chitin dome, which was approximately two feet in diameter. The kragen squirmed and shuddered, whether in pain or apprehension it alone knew. As Sklar Hast worked around to the front, the palps groped back for him, but he shielded himself behind the turret, and finally gouged out the lamellum completely around the circumference of the turret.

His followers watched in awe and silence; from the main float came somber mutters, and occasional whimpers of superstitious dread from the children.

The channel was cut; Sklar Hast handed chisel and mallet back to Elmar Pronave. He mounted the body of the kragen,

* The Advertiserman takes below a pulley which he attaches to a sea-plant stalk. By means of ropes, buckets of air are pulled down, allowing him to remain under water as long as he chooses. Using two such systems, alternately lowered, the diver can descend to a depth of two hundred feet, where the sea-plant stalks grow dense and rigid.

bent his knees, hooked fingers under the edge of the chitin dome, heaved. The dome ripped up and off, almost unbalancing Sklar Hast. The dome rolled down to the pad, the turret stood like an open-topped cylinder; within were coils and loops of something like dirty gray string. There were knots here, nodes there, on each side a pair of kinks, to the front a great tangle of kinks and loops.

Sklar Hast looked down in interest. He was joined by Elmar Pronave. "The creature's brain, evidently," said Sklar Hast. "Here the ganglions terminate. Or perhaps they are merely the termini of muscles."

Elmar Pronave took the mallet and with the handle prodded at a node. The kragen gave a furious jerk. "Well, well," said Pronave. "Interesting indeed." He prodded further: here, there. Every time he touched the exposed ganglions the kragen jerked. Sklar Hast suddenly put out his hand to halt him. "Notice. On the right, those two long loops; likewise on the left. When you touched this one here, the fore-vane jerked." He took the mallet, prodded each of the loops in turn; and in turn each of the vanes jerked.

"Aha!" declared Elmar Pronave. "Should we persist, we could teach the kragen to jig."

"Best we should kill the beast," said Sklar Hast. "Day is approaching and who knows but what..." From the float sounded a sudden low wail, quickly cut off as by the constriction of breath. The group around the kragen stirred; someone vented a deep sound of dismay. Sklar Hast jumped up on the kragen, looked around. The population on the float were staring to sea; he looked likewise, to see King Kragen. He floated under the surface, only his turret above water. The eyes stared forward, each a foot across: lenses of tough crystal behind which flickered milky films and pale blue sheen. King Kragen had either drifted close down the trail of Phocan's Cauldron on the water, or approached sub-surface.

Fifty feet from the lagoon nets he let his bulk come to the surface: first the whole of his turret, then the black cylinder housing the maw and the digestive process, finally the great flat sub-body: this, five feet thick, thirty feet wide, sixty feet long. To the sides protruded the propulsive vanes, thick as the girth of three men. Viewed from dead ahead King Kragen appeared a deformed ogre swimming the breast-stroke. His forward eyes, in their horn tubes, were turned toward the float of Sklar Hast, and seemed fixed upon the hulk of the mutilated kragen. The men stared back, muscles stiff as sea-plant stalk. The kragen which they had captured, once so huge and formidable, now seemed a miniature, a doll, a toy. Through its after-eyes it saw King Kragen, and gave a fluting whistle, a sound completely lost and desolate.

Sklar Hast suddenly found his tongue. He spoke in a husky urgent tone. "Back. To the back of the pad. Swim to the float."

From the main float rose the voice of Semon Voidenvo the Intercessor. In quavering tones he called out across the water: "Behold, King Kragen, the men of Tranque Float! Now we denounce the presumptuous bravado of these few heretics! Behold, this pleasant lagoon, with its succulent sponges, devoted to the well-being of the magnanimous King Kragen—" the reedy voice faltered as King Kragen twitched his great vanes and eased forward. The great eyes stared without discernible expression, but behind there seemed to be a leaping and shifting of pale pink and pale blue lights. The folk on the float drew back as King Kragen breasted close to the net. With a twitch of his vanes, he ripped the net; two more twitches shredded it. From the folk on the float came a moan of dread; King Kragen had not been mollified.

King Kragen eased into the lagoon, approached Sklar Hast's pad which now was deserted except for the helpless kragen. The bound beast thrashed feebly, sounded its fluting whistle. King Kragen reached forth a palp, seized it, lifted it into the air, where it dangled helplessly. King Kragen drew it contemptuously close to his great mandibles, chopped it quickly into slices of gray and black gristle. These he tossed away, out into the ocean. He paused to drift a moment, to consider. Then he surged on Sklar Hast's pad. One blow of his fore-vane demolished the hut, another cut a great gouge in the pad. The after-vanes thrashed among the arbors; water, debris, broken sponges boiled up from below. King Kragen thrust again, wallowed completely up on the pad, which slowly crumpled and sank beneath his weight.

King Kragen pulled himself back into the lagoon, cruised back and forth destroying arbors, shredding the net, smashing huts of all the pads of the lagoon. Then he turned his attention to the main float, breasting up to the edge. For a moment he eyed the population, which started to set up a terrified keening sound, then thrust himself forward, wallowed up on the float, and the keening became a series of hoarse cries and screams. The folk ran back and forth with jerky scurrying steps.

King Kragen bulked on the float like a toad on a lily-pad. He struck with his vanes; the float split. The hoodwink tower, the great structure so cunningly woven, so carefully contrived, tottered. King Kragen lunged again, the tower toppled, falling into the huts along the north edge of the float.

King Kragen floundered across the float. He destroyed the granary, and bushels of yellow meal laboriously scraped from sea-plant pistils streamed into the water. He crushed the racks where stalk, withe and fiber were stretched and flexed; he dealt likewise with the rope-walk. Then, as if suddenly in a hurry, he swung about, heaved himself to the southern edge of the float. A number of huts and thirty-two of the folk, mostly aged and very young, were crushed or thrust into the water and drowned.

King Kragen regained the open sea. He floated quietly a moment or two, palps twitching in the expression of some unknowable emotion. Then he moved his vanes and slid off across the calm ocean.

Tranque Float was a devastation, a tangle, a scene of wrath and grief. The lagoon had returned to the ocean, with the arbors reduced to rubbish and the shoals of food-fish scattered. Many huts had been crushed. The hoodwink tower lay toppled. Of a population of four hundred and eighty, forty-three were dead, with as many more injured. The survivors stood blank-eyed and limp, unable to comprehend the full extent of the disaster which had come upon them.

Presently they roused themselves, and gathered at the far western edge where the damage had been the least. Ixon Myrex sought through the faces, eventually spied Sklar Hast sitting on a fragment of the fallen hoodwink tower. He raised his hand slowly, pointed. "Sklar Hast! I denounce you. The evil you have done to Tranque Float cannot be uttered in words. Your arrogance, your callous indifference to our pleas, your cruel and audacious villainy—how can you hope to expiate them?"

Sklar Hast looked off across the sea.

"In my capacity as Arbiter of Tranque Float, I now declare you to be a criminal of the basest sort, together with all those who served you as accomplices, and most noteworthy Elmar Pronave! Elmar Pronave, show your shameful face! Where do you hide?"

But Elmar Pronave had been drowned and did not answer.

Chaezy Zander limped across the area to stand beside Ixon Myrex. "I likewise denounce Sklar Hast and declare him Assistant Master Hoodwink no longer. He has disgraced his caste and his calling: I hereby eject him from the fellowship of both!"

Semon Voidenvo the Intercessor rose to speak. "Denunciations are not enough. King Kragen, in wreaking his terrible but just vengeance, intended that the primes of the deed should die. I now declare the will of King Kragen to be death, by either strangulation or bludgeoning, of Sklar Hast and all his accomplices."

"Not so fast," said Sklar Hast at last. "It appears to me that a certain confusion is upon us. Two kragen, a large one and small one, have injured us. I, Sklar Hast, and my friends, are those who hoped to protect the float from depredation. We failed. We are not criminals; we are simply not as strong nor as wicked as King Kragen."

"You are aware," Semon Voidenvo persisted, "that King Kragen reserves to himself the duty of guarding us from the lesser kragen? You are aware that in assaulting the kragen, you in effect assaulted King Kragen?"

Sklar Hast considered. "We will need more powerful tools than ropes and chisels to kill King Kragen."

Semon Voidenvo turned away speechless. The people looked apathetically toward Sklar Hast. Few seemed to share the indignation of the elders.

Ixon Myrex sensed the general feeling of misery and fatigue. "This is no time for recrimination. There is work to be done, vast work; all our structures to be rebuilt, our tower rendered operative, our net rewoven. But Sklar Hast's crime must not go without appropriate punishment. I therefore propose a Grand Convocation to take place one week from today, on Apprise Float. The fate of Sklar Hast and his gang will be inexorably decided by a Council of Elders."

CHAPTER ii

THE OCEAN HAD never been plumbed. At two hundred feet, the maximum depth attempted by stalk-cutters and pod-gatherers, the sea-plant stems were still a tangle. One Waller Murven, a man half-daredevil, half-maniac, had descended to three hundred feet, and in the indigo gloom noted the stalks merging to disappear into the murk as a single great trunk. But attempts to sound the bottom, by means of a line weighted with a bag of bone chippings, were unsuccessful. How then had the sea-plants managed to anchor themselves? Some supposed that the plants were of great antiquity, and had developed during a time when the water was much lower. Others conjectured a sinking of the ocean bottom; still others were content to ascribe the feat to an innate tendency of the sea-plants.

Of all the floats Apprise was the largest and one of the first to be settled. The central agglomeration was perhaps seven acres in extent; the lagoon was bounded by thirty or forty smaller pads. Apprise Float was the traditional site of the convocations, which occurred at approximately yearly intervals and which were attended by the active and responsible adults of the system. Drama and excitement attended the holding of the convocations. The folk of the floats seldom ventured far from home, since it was widely believed that King Kragen disapproved of travel. He ignored the coracles of swindlers, and also the rafts of withe or stalk which occasionally passed back and forth between the floats; but on various occasions he had demolished boats or coracles which seemed to have no ostensible business or purpose. Coracles conveying folk to a convocation had never been molested, however, even though King Kragen always seemed aware that a convocation was in progress, and often watched proceedings from a distance of a half-mile or so. How King Kragen gained his knowledge was a matter of great mystery: some asserted that on every float lived a man who was a man in semblance only: who inwardly was a manifestation of King Kragen. It was through this man, according to the superstition, that King Kragen knew what transpired on the floats.

For three days preceding the convocation there was incessant flickering along the line of the hoodwink towers; the destruction of Tranque Float was reported in full detail, together with Ixon Myrex's denunciation of Sklar Hast and Sklar Hast's rebuttal. On each of the floats there was intense discussion and a certain degree of debate. But since, in most cases, the Arbiter and the Intercessor of each float inveighed against Sklar Hast, there was little organized sentiment in his favor.

On the morning of the convocation, early, before the morning sky showed blue, coracles full of folk moved between the floats. The survivors of the Tranque Float disaster, who for the most part had sought refuge on Thrasneck and Bickle, were among the first underway, as were the folk from Almack and Sciona, to the far west.

All morning the coracles shuttled back and forth between the floats; shortly before noon the first groups began to arrive on Apprise. Each group wore the distinctive emblems of its float; and those who felt caste distinction important likewise wore the traditional hair-stylings, forehead plaques and dorsal ribbons; otherwise all dressed in much the same fashion: shirts and pantlets of coarse linen woven from sea-plant fiber; sandals of rug-fish leather, ceremonial gauntlets and epaulettes of sequins cut from the kernels of a certain half-animal, half-vegetable mollusc.

As the folk arrived they trooped to the famous old Apprise Inn where they refreshed themselves at a table on which was set forth a collation of beer, pod-cakes and pickled fingerlings; after which the newcomers separated to various quarters of the float, in accordance with traditional caste distinctions.

In the center of the float was a rostrum and on benches surrounding the notables took their places: craft-masters, caste-chiefs, Arbiters and Intercessors. The rostrum was at all times open to any who wished to speak, so long as they gained the sponsorship of one of the notables. The first speakers at the convocations customarily were elders intent on exhorting the younger folk to excellence and virtue; so it was today. An hour after the sun had reached the zenith the first speaker made his way to the rostrum; a portly old Incendiary from Maudelinda Float who had in just such a fashion opened the speaking at the last five convocations. He sought and was perfunctorily granted sponsorship—by now his speeches were regarded as a necessary evil; he mounted the rostrum and began to speak. His voice was rich, throbbing, voluminous; his periods were long, his sentiments well-used, his illuminations unremarkable:

"We meet again; I am pleased to see so many of the faces which over the years have become familiar and well-beloved; and alas there are certain faces no more to be seen, those who have slipped away to the Bourne, many untimely, as those who suffered punishment only these few days past before the wrath of King Kragen, of which we all stand in awe. A dreadful circumstance thus to provoke the majesty of this Elemental Reality; it should never have occurred; it would never have occurred if all abided by the ancient disciplines. Why must we scorn the wisdom of our ancestors? Those noble and most heroic of men who dared to revolt against the tyranny of the mindless helots, seize the Ship of Space which was taking them to brutal confinement, and seek a haven here on this blessed world! Our ancestors knew the benefits of order and rigor: they designated the castes and set them to tasks for which they presumably had received training on the Home-world. In such a fashion the Swindlers were assigned the task of swindling fish; the Hoodwinks were set to winking hoods; the Incendiaries, among whom I am proud to number myself, wove ropes; while the Bezzlers gave us the Intercessors who have procured the favor and benevolent guardianship of King Kragen.

"Like begets like; characteristics persist and distill: why then are the castes crumbling and giving way to helter-skelter disorder? I appeal to the youth of today: read the old books: the Dicta. Study the artifacts in the Museum, renew your dedication to the system formulated by our forefathers: you have no heritage more precious than your caste identity!"

The old Incendiary spoke on in such a vein for several minutes further, and was succeeded by another old man, a former Hoodwink of good reputation, who worked until films upon his eyes gave one configuration much the look of another. Like the old Incendiary he too urged a more fervent dedication to the old-time values. "I deplore the sloth and pudicity of today's youth! We are becoming a race of sluggards! It is sheer good fortune that King Kragen protects us from the gluttony of the lesser kragen. And what if the tyrants of out-space discovered our haven and sought once more to enslave us? How would we defend ourselves? By hurling fish-heads? By diving under the floats in the hope that our adversaries would follow and drown themselves? I propose that each float form a militia, well-trained and equipped with darts and spears, fashioned from the most durable stalk obtainable!"

The old Hoodwink was followed by the Sumber Float Intercessor, who courteously suggested that should the out-space tyrants appear, King Kragen would be sure to visit upon them the most poignant punishments, the most absolute of rebuffs, so that the tyrants would flee in terror never to return. "King Kragen is mighty, King Kragen is wise and benevolent, unless his dignity is impugned, as in the detestable incident at Tranque Float, where the wilfulness of a bigoted free-thinker caused agony to many." Now he modestly turned down his head. "It is neither my place nor my privilege to propose a punishment suitable to so heinous an offense as the one under discussion. But I would go beyond this particular crime to dwell upon the underlying causes; namely the bravado of certain folk, who ordain themselves equal or superior to the accepted ways of life which have served us so well so long…"

Presently he descended to the float. His place was taken by a somber man of stalwart physique, wearing the plainest of garments. "My name is Sklar Hast," he said. "I am that so-called 'bigoted free-thinker' just referred to. I have much to say, but I hardly know how to say it. I will be blunt. King Kragen is not the wise beneficent guardian the Intercessors like to pretend. King Kragen is a gluttonous beast who every year becomes more enormous and more gluttonous. I sought to kill a lesser kragen which I found destroying my arbors; by some means King Kragen learned of this attempt and reacted with insane malice."

"Hist! Hist!" cried the Intercessors from below. "Shame! Outrage!"

"Why does King Kragen resent my effort? After all, he kills any lesser kragen he discovers in the vicinity. It is simple and self-evident. King Kragen does not want men to think about killing kragen for fear they will attempt to kill him. I propose that this is what we do. Let us put aside this ignoble servility, this groveling to a sea-beast, let us turn our best efforts to the destruction of King Kragen."

"Irresponsible maniac!" "Fool!" "Vile-minded ingrate!" called the Intercessors in wrath.

Sklar Hast waited, but the invective increased in volume. Finally Phyral Berwick the Apprise Arbiter mounted the rostrum and held up his hands. "Quiet! Let Sklar Hast speak! He stands on the rostrum; it is his privilege to say what he wishes."

"Must we listen to garbage and filth?" called Semon Voidenvo. "This man has destroyed Tranque Float; now he urges his frantic lunacy upon the rest of us."

"Let him urge," declared Phyral Berwick. "You are under no obligation to comply."

Sklar Hast said, "The Intercessors naturally resist these ideas; they are bound closely to King Kragen, and claim to have some means of communicating with him. Possibly this is so. Why else should King Kragen arrive so opportunely at Tranque Float? Now here is a very cogent point: if we can agree to liberate ourselves from King Kragen, we must prevent the Intercessors from making known our plans to him, otherwise we shall suffer more than necessary. Most of you know in your hearts that I speak truth. King Kragen is a crafty beast with an insatiable appetite and we are his slaves. You know this truth but you fear to acknowledge it. Those who spoke before me have mentioned our forefathers: the men who captured a ship from the tyrants who sought to immure them on a penal planet. What would our forefathers have done? Would they have submitted to this gluttonous ogre? Of course not.

"How can we kill King Kragen? The plans must wait upon agreement, upon the concerted will to act, and in any event must not be told before the Intercessors. If there are any here who believe as I do, now is the time for them to make themselves heard."

He stepped down from the rostrum. Across the float was silence. Men's faces were frozen. Sklar Hast looked to right and to left. No one met his eye.

Semon Voidenvo mounted the rostrum. "You have listened to the shameless murderer. On Tranque Float we condemned him to death for his malevolent acts. According to custom he demanded the right to speak before a convocation; now he has done so. Has he confessed his great crime; has he wept for the evil he has visited upon Tranque Float? No; he gibbers his plans for further enormities; he outrages decency by mentioning our ancestors in the same breath with his foul proposals. Let the convocation endorse the verdict of Tranque Float; let all those who respect King Kragen and benefit from his ceaseless vigilance, raise now their hands in the clenched fist of death!"

"Death!" roared the Intercessors and raised their fists. But elsewhere through the crowd there was hesitation and uneasiness. Eyes shifted backwards and forwards; there were furtive glances out to sea. Semon Voidenvo once more called for a signal, and now a few fists were raised.

Phyral Berwick, the Apprise Monitor, rose to his feet. "I remind Semon Voidenvo that he has now called twice for the death of Sklar Hast. If he calls once more and fails to achieve an affirmative vote Sklar Hast is vindicated."

Semon Voidenvo's face sagged. He looked uncertainly over the crowd, and without further statement descended.

The rostrum was empty. No one sought to speak. Finally Phyral Berwick himself mounted the steps. He was a stocky square-faced man with gray hair, ice-blue eyes, a short gray beard. He spoke slowly. "You have heard Sklar Hast, who calls for the death of King Kragen. You have heard Semon Voidenvo, who calls for the death of Sklar Hast. I will tell you my feelings. I have great fear in the first case and great disinclination in the second. I have no clear sense of what I should do."

From the audience a man called "Question!" Phyral Berwick nodded. "State your name, caste and craft, and propound your question."

"I am Meth Cagno; I am by blood a Larcener, although I no longer follow caste custom; my craft is that of Scrivener. My question has this background: Sklar Hast has voiced a conjecture which I think deserves an answer: namely, that Semon Voidenvo, the Tranque Intercessor, called King Kragen to Tranque Float. This is a subtle question, because much depends upon not only if Semon Voidenvo issued the call, but precisely when. If he did so when the rogue kragen was first discovered, well and good. But—if he called after Sklar Hast made his attempt to kill the rogue, Semon Voidenvo is more guilty of the Tranque disaster than Sklar Hast. My question then: what is the true state of affairs? Do the Intercessors secretly communicate with King Kragen? Specifically, did Semon Voidenvo call King Kragen to Tranque Float in order that Sklar Hast should be punished?"

Phyral Berwick deliberated. "I cannot answer your question. But I think it deserves an answer. Semon Voidenvo, what do you say?"

"I say nothing."

"Come," said Phyral Berwick reasonably. "Your craft is Intercessor; your responsibility is to the men whom you represent, not to King Kragen, no matter how fervent your respect. Any evasion or secrecy can only arouse our misgivings."

"It is to be understood," said Semon Voidenvo tartly, "that if I did indeed summon King Kragen, my motives were of the highest order."

"Well, then, did you do so?"

Semon Voidenvo cast about for a means to escape from his dilemma, and found none. Finally he said, "There is a means by which the Intercessors are able to summon King Kragen in the event that a rogue kragen appears. This occurred; I so summoned King Kragen."

"Indeed." Phyral Berwick drummed his fingers on the rail of the rostrum. "Are these the only occasions that you summon King Kragen?"

"Why do you question me?" demanded Semon Voidenvo. "I am Intercessor; the criminal is Sklar Hast."

"Easy, then; the questions illuminate the extent of the alleged crime. For instance, let me ask this: do you ever summon King Kragen to feed from your lagoon in order to visit a punishment upon the folk of your float?"

Semon Voidenvo blinked. "The wisdom of King Kragen is inordinate. He can detect delinquencies, he makes his presence known—"

"Specifically then, you summoned King Kragen to Tranque Float when Sklar Hast sought to kill the lesser kragen?"

"My acts are not in the balance. I see no reason to answer the question."

Phyral Berwick spoke to the crowd in a troubled voice. "There seems no way to determine exactly when Semon Voidenvo called King Kragen. If he did so after Sklar Hast had begun his attack upon the rogue, then in my opinion, Semon

Voidenvo the Intercessor is more immediately responsible for the Tranque disaster than Sklar Hast. Thereupon it becomes a travesty to visit any sort of penalty upon Sklar Hast. Unfortunately there seems no way of settling this question."

The Apprise Intercessor, Barquan Blasdel, rose slowly to his feet. "Arbiter Berwick, I fear that you are seriously confused. Sklar Hast and his gang committed an act knowingly proscribed both by the Tranque Monitor Ixon Myrex and by the Tranque Intercessor Semon Voidenvo. The consequences stemmed from this act; hence Sklar Hast is guilty."

"Barquan Blasdel," said Phyral Berwick, "you are Apprise Intercessor. Have you ever summoned King Kragen to Apprise Float?"

"As Semon Voidenvo pointed out, Sklar Hast is the criminal at the bar, not the conscientious intercessors of the various floats. By no means may Sklar Hast be allowed to evade his punishment. King Kragen is not lightly to be defied. Even though the convocation will not raise their collective fist to smite Sklar Hast, I say that he must die."

Phyral Berwick fixed his pale blue eyes upon Barquan Blasdel. "If the convocation gives Sklar Hast his life, he will not die unless I die before him."

Meth Cagno came forward. "And I likewise."

The men of Tranque Float who had joined Sklar Hast in the killing of the rogue kragen came toward the rostrum, shouting their intention of joining Sklar Hast either in life or death, and with them came others, from various floats.

Barquan Blasdel climbed onto the rostrum, held his hands wide. "Before others declare themselves—look out to sea. King

Kragen watches, attentive to learn who is loyal and who is faithless."

The crowd swung about as if one individual. A hundred yards off the float the water swirled lazily around King Kragen's great turret. The crystal eyes pointed like telescopes toward Apprise Float. Presently the turret sank beneath the surface. The blue water roiled, then flowed smooth and featureless.

Sklar Hast went to the ladder, started to mount to the rostrum. Barquan Blasdel the Intercessor halted him. "The rostrum must not become a shouting-place. Stay till you are summoned!" But Sklar Hast pushed him aside, went to face the crowd. He pointed toward the smooth ocean. "There you have seen the vile beast, our enemy! Why should we deceive ourselves? Intercessors, Arbiters, all of us—let us forget our differences, let us join our crafts and our resources! If we do so, we can evolve a method to kill King Kragen! So now—decide!"

Barquan Blasdel threw back his head aghast. He took a step toward Sklar Hast, as if to seize him, then turned to the audience. "You have heard this madman—twice you have heard him. You have also observed the vigilance of King Kragen whose force is known to all. You can choose therefore either to obey the exhortations of a twitching lunatic, or be guided by your ancient trust in the benevolence of mighty King Kragen. In one manner only does Sklar Hast speak truth: there must be a definite resolution to this matter. We can have no half-measures! Sklar Hast must die! So now hold high your fists—each and all! Silence the frantic screamings of Sklar Hast! King Kragen is near at hand! Death to Sklar Hast!" He thrust his fist high into the air.

The Intercessors followed suit. "Death to Sklar Hast!"

Hesitantly, indecisively, other fists raised, then others and others. Some changed their minds and drew down their fists; others submitted to arguments and either drew down their fists or thrust them high; some raised their fists only to have others pull them down. Altercations sprang up across the float; the hoarse sound of contention began to make itself heard. Barquan Blasdel leaned forward in sudden concern, calling for calm. Sklar Hast likewise started to speak, but he desisted—because suddenly words were of no avail. In a bewildering, almost magical, shift the placid convocation had become a mêlée. Men and women tore savagely at each other, screaming, cursing, raging, squealing. Emotion accumulated from childhood, stored and constrained, had suddenly exploded; and the identical fear and hate had prompted opposite reactions. Across the float the tide of battle surged, out into the water where staid Bezzlers and responsible Larceners sought to drown each other. Few weapons were available: clubs of stalk, a bone axe or two, a half-dozen stakes, as many knives. While the struggle was at its most intense King Kragen once more surfaced, this time a quarter mile to the north from whence he turned his vast incurious gaze upon the float.

The fighting slowed and dwindled, from sheer exhaustion. The combatants drew apart into panting bleeding groups. In the lagoon floated half-a-dozen corpses; on the float lay as many more. Now for the first time it could be seen that those who stood by Sklar Hast were considerably outnumbered, by almost two to one, and also that this group included for the most part the most vigorous and able of the craftsmen, though few of the Masters: about half of the Hoodwinks, two-thirds of the Scriveners, relatively few from the Jacklegs, Advertisermen, Nigglers and other low castes, fewer still of the Arbiters and no Intercessors whatever.

Barquan Blasdel, still on the rostrum, cried out, "This is a sorry day indeed; a sorry day! Sklar Hast, see the anguish you have brought to the floats! There can be no mercy for you now!"

Sklar Hast came forward, pale and flaming-eyed. Blood coursed down his face from the slash of a knife. Ignoring Blasdel he mounted the rostrum, and addressed the two groups:

"As Blasdel the Intercessor has said, there is no turning back now. So be it. Let those who want to serve King Kragen remain. Let those who want free lives go forth across the sea. There are floats to north and south, to east and west, floats as kind and hospitable as these, where we will soon have homes as rich and modern—perhaps more so."

Barquan Blasdel strode forward. "Go then! All you faithless, you irreverent ones—get hence and good riddance! Go where you will, and never seek to return when the teeming kragen, unchided by the great King, devour your sponges, tear your nets, crush your coracles!"

"The many cannot be as rapacious as the one," said Sklar Hast. "You who will go then, return to your floats, load tools and cordage, all your utile goods into your coracles. In two days we depart. Our destination and other details must remain secret. I need not explain why." He cast an ironic look toward Barquan Blasdel.

"You need not fear our interference," said Blasdel. "You may depart at will; indeed we will facilitate your going."

"On the morning of the third day hence, then, when the wind blows fair, we depart."

CHAPTER iii

BARQUAN BLASDEL THE Apprise Intercessor, his spouse and six daughters, occupied a pad to the north of the main float, somewhat isolated and apart. It was perhaps the choicest and most pleasant pad of the Apprise complex, situated where Blasdel could read the hoodwink towers of Apprise, of Quatrefoil and the Bandings to the east, of Granolt to the west. The pad was delightfully overgrown with a hundred different plants and vines: some yielding resinous pods, others capsules of fragrant sap, others crisp tendrils and shoots. Certain shrubs produced stains and pigment; a purple-leaved epiphyte yielded a rich-flavored pith. Other growths were entirely ornamental—a situation not too usual along the floats, where space was at a premium and every growing object weighed for its utility. Along the entire line of floats few pads could compare to that of Barquan Blasdel for beauty, variety of plantings, isolation and calm.

In late afternoon of the second day after the turbulent convocation, Barquan Blasdel returned to his pad. He dropped the
painter of his coracle over a stake of carved bone, gazed ap-
preciatively into the west. The sun had only just departed the
sky, which now glowed with effulgent greens, blues, and, at the
zenith, a purple of exquisite purity. The ocean, shuddering to
the first whispers of the evening breeze, reflected the sky. Blasdel
felt surrounded, immersed in color...He turned away, marched
to his house, whistling a complacent tune between his teeth.
On the morrow the most troublesome elements of all the floats
would depart on the morning breeze, and no more would be
heard from them ever. And Blasdel's whistling became slow and
thoughtful. Although life flowed smoothly and without contention, over the years a certain uneasiness and dissatisfaction had
begun to make itself felt. Dissident elements had begun to question the established order. The sudden outbreak of violence at
the convocation perhaps had been inevitable: an explosion of
suppressed or even unconscious tensions. But all was working
out for the best. The affair could not have resolved itself more
smoothly if he had personally arranged the entire sequence
of events. At one stroke all the skeptics, grumblers, ne'er-
do-wells, the covertly insolent, the obstinate hard-heads—at
one stroke, all would disappear, never again to trouble the easy
and orthodox way of life.

Almost jauntily Barquan Blasdel ambled up the path to his
residence: a group of five semi-detached huts, screened by the
garden from the main float, and so providing a maximum of
privacy for Blasdel, his spouse and his six daughters. Blasdel
halted. On a bench beside the door sat a man. Twilight murk

concealed his face. Blasdel frowned, peered. Intruders upon his private pad were not welcome. Blasdel marched forward. The man rose from the bench and bowed: it was Phyral Berwick, the Apprise Arbiter. "Good evening," said Berwick. "I trust I did not startle you."

"By no means," said Blasdel shortly. With rank equal to his own Berwick could not be ignored, although after his unconventional actions at the convocation Blasdel could not bring himself to display more than a minimum of formal courtesy. He said, "Unfortunately I was not expecting callers and can offer you no refreshment."

"A circumstance of no moment," declared Berwick. "I desire neither food nor drink." He waved his hand around the pad. "You live on a pad of surpassing beauty, Barquan Blasdel. There are many who might envy you."

Blasdel shrugged. "Since my conduct is orthodox, I am armored against adverse opinion. But what urgency brings you here? I fear that I must be less than ceremonious; I am shortly due at the hoodwink tower to participate in a coded all-float conference."

Berwick made a gesture of polite acquiescence. "My business is of small moment. But I would not keep you standing out here in the dusk. Shall we enter?"

Blasdel grunted, opened the door, allowed Berwick to enter. From a cupboard he brought luminant fiber, which he set aglow and arranged in a holder. Turning a quick side-glance toward Berwick he said, "In all candor I am somewhat surprised to see you. Apparently you were among the most vehement of those dissidents who planned to depart."

"I may well have given that impression," Berwick agreed. "But you must realize that declarations uttered in the heat of emotion are occasionally amended in the light of sober reason."

Blasdel nodded curtly. "True enough. I suspect that many of the ingrates will think twice before joining this hare-brained expedition."

"This is partly the reason for my presence here," said Berwick. He looked around the room. "An interesting chamber. You own dozens of valuable artifacts. But where are the others of your family?"

"In the domestic area. This is my sanctum, my workroom, my place of meditation."

"Indeed." Berwick inspected the walls. "Indeed, indeed! I believe I notice certain relicts of the forefathers!"

"True," said Blasdel. "This small flat object is of the substance called 'metal', and is extremely hard. The best bone knife will not scratch it. The purpose of this particular object I cannot conjecture. It is an heirloom. These books are exact copies of the Dicta in the Hall of Archives, and present the memoirs of the Forefathers. Alas! I find them beyond my comprehension. There is nothing more of any great interest. On the shelf—my ceremonial head-dresses; you have seen them before. Here is my telescope. It is old; the case is warped, the gum of the lenses has bulged and cracked. It was poor gum, to begin with. But I have little need for a better instrument. My possessions are few. Unlike many Intercessors and certain Arbiters," here he cast a meaningful eye at Phyral Berwick, "I do not choose to surround myself with sybaritical cushions and baskets of sweetmeats."

Berwick laughed ruefully. "You have touched upon my

weaknesses. Perhaps the fear of deprivation has occasioned second-thoughts in me."

"Ha hah!" Blasdel became jovial. "I begin to understand. The scalawags who set off to wild new floats can expect nothing but hardship: wild fish, horny sponges, new varnish with little more body than water; in short they will be returning to the life of savages. They must expect to suffer the depredations of lesser kragen, who will swiftly gather. Perhaps in time…" His voice dwindled, his face took on a thoughtful look.

"What was it you were about to say?" prompted Phyral Berwick.

Blasdel gave a non-committal laugh. "An amusing, if far-fetched, conceit crossed my mind. Perhaps in time one of these lesser kragen will vanquish the others, and drive them away. When this occurs, those who flee King Kragen will have a king of their own, who may eventually…" Again his voice paused.

"Who may eventually rival King Kragen in size and force?" Berwick supplied. "The concept is not unreasonable—although King Kragen is already enormous from long feasting, and shows no signs of halting his growth." An almost imperceptible tremor moved the floor of the hut. Blasdel went to look out the door. "I thought I felt the arrival of a coracle."

"Conceivably a gust of wind," said Berwick. "Well, to my errand. As you have guessed I did not come to examine your relics or comment upon the comfort of your cottage. My business is this. I feel a certain sympathy for those who are leaving, and I feel that no one, not even the most violently fanatic Intercessor, would wish this group to meet King Kragen upon the ocean. King Kragen, as you are aware, disapproves of exploration, and becomes petulant, even wrathful, when he finds men venturing out upon the ocean. Perhaps he fears the possibility of the second King Kragen concerning which we speculated. Hence I came to inquire the whereabouts of King Kragen. In the morning the wind blows east, and the optimum location for King Kragen would be to the far east at Tranque or Thrasneck."

Blasdel nodded sagely. "The emigrants are putting their luck to the test. Should King Kragen chance to be waiting in the east tomorrow morning, and should he spy the flotilla, his wrath might well be excited, to the detriment of the expedition."

"And where," inquired Berwick, "was King Kragen at last notification?"

Barquan Blasdel knit his brows. "I believe I noted a hoodwink message to the effect that he was seen cruising in a westerly direction to the south of Bickle Float, toward Maudelinda. I might well have misread the flicker, I only noted the configuration from the corner of my eye—but such was my understanding."

"Excellent," declared Berwick. "This is good news. The emigrants should make their departure safely and without interference."

"So we hope," said Blasdel. "King Kragen of course is subject to unpredictable whims and quirks."

Berwick made a confidential sign. "Sometimes—so it is rumored—he responds to signals transmitted in some mysterious manner by the Intercessors. Tell me, Barquan Blasdel, is this the case? We are both notables and together share responsibility for the welfare of Apprise Float. Is it true then that the Intercessors communicate with King Kragen, as has been alleged?"

"Now then, Arbiter Berwick," said Blasdel, "this is hardly a pertinent question. Should I answer yes, then I would be divulging a craft secret. Should I answer no, then it would seem that we Intercessors boast of nonexistent capabilities. So you must satisfy yourself with those hypotheses which seem the most profitable."

"Fairly answered," said Phyral Berwick. "However—and in the strictest confidence—I will report to you an amusing circumstance. As you know, at the convocation I declared myself for the party of Sklar Hast. Subsequently I was accepted into their most intimate counsels. I can inform you with authority—but first, you will assure me of your silence? As under no circumstances would I betray Sklar Hast or compromise the expedition."

"Certainly, indeed; my lips are sealed as with fourteen-year old varnish."

"Well then, I accept you at your word. This is Sklar Hast's amusing tactic: he has arranged that a group of influential Intercessors shall accompany the group. If all goes well, the Intercessors live. If not, like all the rest, they are crushed in the mandibles of King Kragen." And Phyral Berwick, standing back, watched Barquan Blasdel with an attentive gaze. "What do you make of that?"

Blasdel stood rigid, fingering his fringe of black beard. He darted a quick glance toward Berwick. "Which Intercessors are to be kidnaped?"

"Aha," said Berwick. "That, like the response of the question I put to you, is in the nature of a craft secret. I doubt if lesser men will be troubled, but if I were Intercessor for Aumerge, or

Sumber, or Quatrefoil, or even Apprise, I believe that I might have cause for caution."

Blasdel stared at Berwick with mingled suspicion and uneasiness. "Do you take this means to warn me? If so, I would thank you to speak less ambiguously. Personally I fear no such attack. Within a hundred feet are three stalwarts, testing my daughters for marriage. A loud call would bring instant help from the float, which is scarcely a stone's throw beyond the garden."

Berwick nodded sagely. "It seems then that you are utterly secure."

"Still, I must hurry to the float," said Blasdel. "I am expected at a conference, and the evening grows no younger."

Berwick bowed and stood aside. "You will naturally remember to reveal nothing of what I told you, to vouchsafe no oblique warning, to hint nothing of the matter—in fact to make no reference to it whatever."

Blasdel considered. "I will say nothing beyond my original intention, to the effect that the villain Sklar Hast obviously knows no moderation, and that it behooves all notables and craft masters to guard themselves against some form of final vengeance."

Berwick paused. "I hardly think you need go quite so far. Perhaps you could phrase it somewhat differently. In this wise: Sklar Hast and his sturdy band take their leave in the morning; now is the last chance for persons so inclined to cast in their lot with the group; however, you hope that all Intercessors will remain at their posts."

"Pah," cried Barquan Blasdel indignantly. "That conveys no sense of imminence. I will say, Sklar Hast is desperate; should he decide to take hostages, his diseased mind would select Intercessors as the most appropriate persons."

Berwick made a firm dissent. "This, I believe, transcends the line I have drawn. My honor is at stake and I can agree to no announcement which baldly states the certainty as a probability. If you choose to make a jocular reference, or perhaps urge that not too many Intercessors join the expedition, then all is well: a subtle germ of suspicion has been planted, you have done your duty and my honor has not been compromised."

"Yes, yes," cried Blasdel, "I agree to anything. But I must hurry to the hoodwink tower. While we quibble Sklar Hast and his bandits are kidnaping Intercessors."

"And what is the harm there?" inquired Berwick mildly. "You state that King Kragen has been observed from Bickle Float proceeding to the west; hence the Intercessors are in no danger, and presumably will be allowed to return once Sklar Hast is assured that King Kragen is no longer a danger. Conversely, if the Intercessors have betrayed Sklar Hast and given information to King Kragen so that he waits off Tranque Float, then they deserve to die with the rest. It is justice of the most precise and exquisite balance."

"That is the difficulty," muttered Blasdel, trying to push past Berwick to the door. "I cannot answer for the silence of the other Intercessors. Suppose one among them has notified King Kragen? Then a great tragedy ensues."

"Interesting! So you can indeed summon King Kragen when you so desire?"

"Yes, yes, but, mind you, this is a secret. And now—"

"It follows then that you always know the whereabouts of King Kragen. How do you achieve this?"

"There is no time to explain; suffice it to say that a means is at hand."

"Right here? In your workroom?"

"Yes indeed. Now stand aside. After I have broadcast the warning I will make all clear. Stand aside then!"

Berwick shrugged and allowed Blasdel to run from the cottage, through the garden to the edge of the pad.

Blasdel stopped short at the water's edge. The coracle had disappeared. Where previously Apprise Float had raised its foliage and its great hoodwink tower against the dusk, there was now only blank water and blank sky. The pad floated free; urged by the west wind of evening it already had left Apprise Float behind.

Blasdel gave an inarticulate cry of fury and woe. He turned to find Berwick standing behind him. "What has happened?"

"It seems that while we talked, divers cut through the stem of your pad. At least this is my presumption."

"Yes, yes," grated Blasdel. "So much is obvious. What else?"

Berwick shrugged. "It appears that willy-nilly, whether we like it or not, we are part of the great emigration. Now that such is the case I am relieved to know that you have a means to determine the whereabouts of King Kragen. Come. Let us make use of this device and reassure ourselves."

Blasdel made a guttural sound deep in his throat. He crouched and for a moment appeared on the point of hurling himself at Phyral Berwick. From the shadows of the verdure appeared another man. Berwick pointed. "I believe Sklar Hast himself is at hand."

"You tricked me," groaned Barquan Blasdel between clenched teeth. "You have performed an infamous act, which you shall regret."

"I have done no such deed, although it appears that you may well have misunderstood my position. Still, the time for recrimination is over. We share a similar problem, which is how to escape the malevolence of King Kragen. I suggest that you now proceed to locate him."

Without a word Blasdel turned, proceeded to his cottage. He entered the main room, with Berwick and Sklar Hast close behind. He crossed to the wall, lifted a panel to reveal an inner room. He brought more lights; all entered. A hole had been cut in the floor, and through the pad, the spongy tissue having been painted with a black varnish to prevent its growing together. A tube fashioned from fine yellow stalk perhaps four inches in diameter led down into the water. "At the bottom," said Blasdel curtly, "is a carefully devised horn, of exact shape and quality. The end is four feet in diameter and covered with a diaphragm of seasoned and varnished pad-skin. King Kragen emits a sound to which this horn is sensitive." He went to the tube, put down his ear, listened, slowly turned the tube around a vertical axis. He shook his head. "I hear nothing. This means that King Kragen is at least ten miles distant. If he is closer I can detect him. He passed to the east early today; presumably he swims somewhere near Sumber, or Adelvine."

Sklar Hast laughed quietly. "Urged there by the Intercessors?"

Blasdel shrugged sourly. "As to that I have nothing to say."

"How then do you summon King Kragen?"

Blasdel pointed to a rod rising from the floor, the top of which terminated in a crank. "In the water below is a drum. Inside this drum fits a wheel. When the crank is turned, the wheel, working in resin, rubs against the drum and emits a signal. King Kragen can sense this sound from a great distance— once again about ten miles. When he is needed, at say Bickle Float, the Intercessor at Aumerge calls him, until the horn reveals him to be four or five miles distant, whereupon the Intercessor at Paisley calls him a few miles, then the Maudelinda Intercessor, and so forth until he is within range of the Intercessor at Bickle Float."

Sklar Hast nodded. "I see. In this fashion Semon Voidenvo called King Kragen to Tranque. Whereupon King Kragen destroyed Tranque Float and killed forty-three persons."

"That is the case."

Sklar Hast turned away. Phyral Berwick told Blasdel, "I believe that Semon Voidenvo is one of the Intercessors who are accompanying the emigration. His lot may not be a happy one."

"This is unreasonable," Barquan Blasdel declared heatedly. "He was as faithful to his convictions as Sklar Hast is to his own. After all, Voidenvo did not enjoy the devastation of Tranque Float. It is his home. Many of those killed were his friends. But he gives his faith and trust to King Kragen."

Sklar Hast swung around. "And you?"

Blasdel shook his head. "Not with such wholeheartedness."

Sklar Hast looked toward Berwick. "What should we do with this apparatus? Destroy it? Or preserve it?"

Berwick considered. "We might on some occasion wish to listen for King Kragen. I doubt if we ever will desire to summon him."

Sklar Hast gave a sardonic jerk of the head. "Who knows? To his death perhaps." He turned to Blasdel. "What persons are aboard the pad in addition to us?"

"My spouse—in the cottage two roofs along. Three young daughters who weave ornaments for the Star-cursing Festival. Three older daughters are attempting to prove themselves to three stalwarts who test them for wives. All are unaware that their home floats out on the deep ocean. None wish to become emigrants to a strange line of floats."

Sklar Hast said, "No more were any of the rest of us—until we were forced to choose. I feel no pity for them, or for you. Undoubtedly there will be ample work for all hands. Indeed, we may formulate a new guild: the Kragen-killers. If rumor is accurate, they infest the ocean."

He left the room, went out into the night. Blasdel cast a wry look at Phyral Berwick, went to listen once more at the detecting horn. Then he likewise left the room. Berwick followed, and lowered the panel. Both joined Sklar Hast at the edge of the pad, where now several coracles were tied. A dozen men stood in the garden. Sklar Hast turned to Blasdel. "Summon your spouse, your daughters and those who test them. Explain the circumstances, and gather your belongings. The evening breeze will soon die and we cannot tow the pad."

Blasdel departed, accompanied by Berwick. Sklar Hast and the others entered the work-room, carried everything of value or utility to the coracles, including the small metal relict, the Books of Dicta, the listening horn and the summoning drum. Then all embarked in the coracles, and Barquan Blasdel's beautiful pad was left to drift solitary upon the ocean.

CHAPTER iv

MORNING CAME TO the ocean and with it the breeze from the west. The floats could no longer be seen; the ocean was a blue mirror in all directions. Sklar Hast lowered Blasdel's horn into the water, listened. Nothing could be heard. Barquan Blasdel did the same and agreed that King Kragen was nowhere near.

There were perhaps six hundred coracles in the flotilla, each carrying from four to eight persons, with as much gear, household equipment and tools as possible, together with sacks of food and water.

Late in the afternoon they noted a few medium-sized floats to the north, but made no attempt to land. King Kragen was yet too near at hand.

The late afternoon breeze arose. Rude sails were rigged and the oarsmen rested. At dusk Sklar Hast ordered all the coracles connected by lines to minimize the risk of separation. When the breeze died and seas reflected the dazzling stars, the sails were brought down and all slept.

The following day was like the first, and also the day after. On the morning of the fourth day a line of splendid floats appeared ahead, easily as large and as rich of foliage as those they had left. Sklar Hast would have preferred to sail on another week, but the folk among the coracles were fervent in their rejoicing, and he clearly would have encountered near-unanimous opposition. So the flotilla landed upon three closely adjoining floats, drove stakes into the pad surface, tethered the coracles.

Sklar Hast called an informal convocation. "In a year or two," he said, "we can live lives as comfortable as those we left behind us. But this is not enough. We left our homes because of King Kragen, who is now our deadly enemy. We shall never rest secure until we find a means to make ourselves supreme over all the kragen. To this purpose we must live different lives than we did in the old days—until King Kragen is killed. How to kill King Kragen? I wish I knew. He is a monster, impregnable to any weapon we now can use against him. So this must be our primary goal: weapons against King Kragen." Sklar Hast paused, looked around the somber group. "This is my personal feeling. I have no authority over any of you, beyond that of the immediate circumstances, which are transient. You have a right to discredit me, to think differently—in which case I will muster those who feel as I do, and sail on to still another float, where we can dedicate ourselves to the killing of King Kragen. If we are all agreed, that our souls are not our own until King

Kragen is dead, then we must formalize this feeling. Authority must be given to some person or group of persons. Responsibilities must be delegated; work must be organized. As you see I envision a life different to the old. It will be harder in some respects, easier in others. First of all, we need not feed King Kragen..."

A committee of seven members was chosen, to serve as a temporary governing body until the needs of the new community required a more elaborate system. As a matter of course Sklar Hast was named to the committee, as well as Phyral Berwick who became the first chairman, and also Meth Cagno the Scrivener. The captured Intercessors sat aside in a sullen group and took no part in the proceedings.

The committee met for an hour, and as its first measure, ordained a census, that each man's caste and craft might be noted.

After the meeting Meth Cagno took Sklar Hast aside. "When you captured Barquan Blasdel, you brought his books."

"True."

"I have been examining these books. They are a set of the Ancient Dicta."

"So I understand."

"This is a source of great satisfaction to me. No one except the Scrivener reads the Dicta nowadays, though everyone professes familiarity. As the generations proceed, the lives of our ancestors and the fantastic environment from which they came seem more like myth than reality."

"I suppose this is true enough. I am a hoodwink by trade and only know hoodwink configurations. The Dicta are written in ancient calligraph, which puzzles me."

"It is difficult to read, that I grant," said Cagno. "However, a patient examination of the Dicta can be profitable. Each volume represents the knowledge of one of our ancestors, to the extent that he was able to organize it. There is also a great deal of repetition and dullness; our ancestors, whatever their talents, had few literary skills. Some are vainglorious and devote pages to self-encomium. Others are anxious to explain in voluminous detail the vicissitudes which led to their presence on the Ship of Space. They seem to have been a very mixed group, from various levels of society. There are hints here and there which I, for one, do not understand. Some describe the Home World as a place of maniacs. Others seem to have held respected places in this society until, as they explain it, the persons in authority turned on them and instituted a savage persecution, ending, as we know, in our ancestors seizing control of the Ship of Space and fleeing to this planet."

"It is all very confusing," said Sklar Hast, "and none of it seems to have much contemporary application. For instance, they do not tell us how they boiled varnish on the Home World, or how they propelled their coracles. Do creatures like the kragen infest the Home World? If so, how do the Home Folk deal with them? Do they kill them or feed them sponges? Our ancestors are silent on these points."

Meth Cagno shrugged. "Evidently they were not overly concerned, or they would have dealt with these matters at length. But I agree that there is much they fail to make clear. As in our own case, the various castes seemed trained to explicit trades. Especially interesting are the memoirs of James Brunet. His caste, that of Counterfeiter, is now extinct among us. Most of his Dicta are rather conventional exhortations to virtue, but toward the middle of the book he says this." Here Cagno opened a book and read:

To those who follow us, to our children and grandchildren, we can leave no tangible objects of value. We brought nothing to the world but ourselves and the wreckage of our lives. We will undoubtedly die here—a fate probably preferable to New Ossining, but by no means the destiny any of us had planned for ourselves. There is no way to escape. Of the entire group I alone have a technical education, most of which I have forgotten. And to what end could I turn it? This is a soft world. It consists of ocean and sea-weed. There is land nowhere. To escape—even if we had the craft to build a new ship, which we do not—we need metal and metal there is none. Even to broadcast a radio signal we need metal. None... No clay to make pottery, no silica for glass, no limestone for concrete, no ore from which to smelt metal. Presumably the ocean carries various salts, but how to extract the metal without electricity? There is iron in our blood: how to extract it? A strange helpless sensation to live on this world where the hardest substance is our own bone! We have, during our lives, taken so many things for granted, and now it seems that no one can evoke something from nothing... This is a problem on which I must think. An ingenious man can work wonders, and I, a successful counterfeiter—or, rather, almost successful— am certainly ingenious.

Meth Cagno paused in his reading. "This is the end of the chapter."

"He seems to be a man of no great force," mused Sklar Hast. "It is true that metal can be found nowhere." He took the bit of metal from his pocket which had once graced the work-room of Barquan Blasdel. "This is obdurate stuff indeed, and perhaps it is what we need to kill King Kragen."

Meth Cagno returned to the book. "He writes his next chapter after a lapse of months:

I have considered the matter at length. But before I proceed I must provide as best I can a picture of the way the universe works, for it is clear that none of my colleagues are in any position to do so, excellent fellows though they are. Please do not suspect me of whimsey: our personalities and social worth undoubtedly vary with the context in which we live.

Here Cagno looked up. "I don't completely understand his meaning here. But I suppose that the matter is -unimportant." He turned the pages. "He now goes into an elaborate set of theorizations regarding the nature of the world, which, I confess, I don't understand. There is small consistency to his beliefs. Either he knows nothing, or is confused, or the world essentially is inconsistent. He claims that all matter is composed of less than a hundred 'elements', joined together in 'compounds'. The elements are constructed of smaller entities: 'electrons', 'protons', 'neutrons', which are not necessarily matter, but forces, depending on your point of view. When electrons move the result is an electric current: a substance or condition—he is not clear here—of great energy and many capabilities. Too much electricity is fatal; in smaller quantities we use it to control our bodies. According to Brunet all sorts of remarkable things can be achieved with electricity."

"Let us provide ourselves an electric current then," said Sklar Hast. "This may become our weapon against the kragen."

"The matter is not so simple. In the first place the electricity must be channeled through metal wires."

"Here is metal," said Sklar Hast, tossing to Meth Cagno the bit of metal he had taken from Blasdel, "though it is hardly likely to be enough."

"The electricity must also be generated," said Cagno, "which on the Home Planet seems to be a complicated process, requiring a great deal of metal."

"Then how do we get metal?"

"On other planets there seems to be no problem. Ore is refined and shaped into a great variety of tools. Here we have no ore. In other cases, metals are extracted from the sea, once again using electricity."

"Hmph," said Sklar Hast. "To procure metal, one needs electricity. To obtain the electricity, metal is required. It seems a closed circle, into which we are unable to break."

Cagno made a dubious face. "It may well be. Brunet mentions various means to generate electricity. There is the 'voltaic cell'—in which two metals are immersed in acid, and he describes a means to generate the acid, using water, brine, and electricity. Then there is thermo-electricity, photo-electricity, chemical electricity, electricity produced by the Rous effect, electricity generated by moving a wire near another wire in which electricity flows. He states that all living creatures produce small quantities of electricity."

"Electricity seems rather a difficult substance to obtain," mused Sklar Hast. "Are there no simple methods to secure metal?"

"Brunet mentions that blood contains a small quantity of iron. He suggests a method for extracting it, by using a high degree of heat. But he also points out that there is at hand no substance capable of serving as a receptacle under such extremes of heat. He states that on the Home World many plants concentrate metallic compounds, and suggests that certain of the sea-plants might do the same. But again either heat or electricity are needed to secure the pure metal."

Sklar Hast ruminated. "Our first and basic problem, as I see it, is self-protection. In short we need a weapon to kill King Kragen. It might be a device of metal—or it might be a larger and more savage kragen, if such exist…" He considered. "Perhaps you should make production of metal and electricity your goal, and let no other pursuits distract you. I am sure that the council will agree, and put at your disposal such helpers as you may need."

"I would gladly do my best."

"And I," said Sklar Hast, "I will reflect upon the kragen."

◶◀◎

Three days later the first kragen was seen, a beast of not inconsiderable size, perhaps twenty feet in length. It came cruising along the edge of the float, and observing the men, stopped short and for twenty minutes floated placidly, swirling water back and forth with its vanes. Then slowly it swung about and continued along the line of floats.

By this time a large quantity of stalk and withe had been cut, scraped and racked, as well as a heap of root-wisp, to cure during the rigging of a rope-walk. A week later the new rope was being woven into net.

Two large pads were cut from the side of the float, stripped of rib-trussing, upper and lower membrane, then set adrift. The space thus opened would become a lagoon. Over the severed stalks sleeves were fitted with one end above water; the sap presently exuding would be removed, boiled and aged for varnish and glue. Meanwhile arbors were constructed, seeded with sponge-floss, and lowered into the lagoon. When the withe had cured, hut-frames were constructed, pad membrane stretched over the mesh and daubed inside and out with varnish.

In a month the community had achieved a rude measure of comfort. On four occasions kragen had passed by, and the fourth occurrence seemed to be a return visit of the first. On this fourth visit the kragen paused, inspected the lagoon with care. It tentatively nudged the net, backed away and presently floated off.

Sklar Hast watched the occurrence, went to inspect the new-cut stalk, which now was sufficiently cured. He laid out a pattern and work began. First a wide base was built near the mouth of the lagoon, with a substructure extending down to the main stem of the float. On this base was erected an A-frame derrick of glued withe, seventy feet tall, with integral braces, the entire structure whipped tightly with strong line and varnished. Another identical derrick was built to over-hang the ocean. Before either of the derricks were completed a small kragen broke through the net to feast upon the yet unripe sponges. Sklar Hast laughed grimly at the incident. "At your next visit, you will not fare so well," he called to the beast. "May the sponges rot in your stomach!"

The kragen swam lazily off down the line of floats, unper-turbed by the threat. It returned two days later. This time the derricks were guyed and in place, but not yet fitted with tackle. Again Sklar Hast reviled the beast, which this time ate with greater fastidiousness, plucking only those sponges which like popcorn had overgrown their husks. The men worked far into the night installing the strut which, when the derrick tilted out over the water, thrust high the topping-halyard to provide greater leverage.

On the next day the kragen returned, and entered the la-goon with insulting assurance: a beast somewhat smaller than that which Sklar Hast had captured on Tranque Float, but none-theless a creature of respectable size. Standing on the float a stalwart old swindler flung a noose around the creature's turret, and on the pad a line of fifty men marched away with a heavy rope. The astonished kragen was towed to the outward leaning derrick, swung up and in. The dangling vanes were lashed; it was lowered to the float. As soon as the bulk collapsed the watching folk, crying out in glee, shoved forward, almost danc-ing into the gnashing mandibles. "Back, fools!" roared Sklar Hast. "Do you want to be cut in half? Back!" He was largely ignored. A dozen chisels hacked at the horny hide; clubs bat-tered at the eyes. "Back!" raged Sklar Hast. "Back! What do you achieve by antics such as this? Back!" Daunted, the vengeful folk moved aside. Sklar Hast took chisel and mallet and as he had done on Tranque Float, cut at the membrane joining dome to turret. He was joined by four others; the channel was swiftly cut and a dozen hands ripped away the dome. Again, with pitiless outcry, the crowd surged forward. Sklar Hast's efforts to halt them were fruitless. The nerves and cords of the creature's ganglionic center were torn from the turret, while the kragen jerked and fluttered and made a buzzing sound with its mandibles. The turret was plucked clean of the wet-string fibers as well as other organs, and the kragen lay limp. Sklar Hast moved away in disgust. Another member of the Seven, Nicklas Rile, stepped forward: "Halt now—no more senseless hacking! If the kragen has bones harder than our own, we will want to preserve them for use. Who knows what use can be made of a kragen's cadaver? The hide is tough; the mandibles are harder than the deepest stalk. Let us proceed intelligently!"

Sklar Hast watched from a little distance as the crowd examined the dead beast. He had no further interest in the kragen. A planned experiment had been foiled almost as soon as the hate driven mob had rushed forward. But there would be more kragen for his derricks; hopefully they could be noosed by the sea-derrick before they broke into the lagoon. In years to come, strong-boats or barges equipped with derricks might even go forth to hunt the kragen…He approached the kragen once again, peered into the empty turret, where now welled a viscous milky blue fluid. James Brunet, in his Dicta, had asserted that the metal iron was a constituent of human blood; conceivably other metals or metallic compounds might be discovered in the blood of a kragen. He found Meth Cagno, who had been watching from a dignified distance, and communicated his hypothesis. Cagno made no dissent. "It may well be the case. Our basic problem, however, remains as before: separating the metal from the dross."

"You have no idea how to proceed?"

Meth Cagno smiled slightly. "I have one or two ideas. In fact, tomorrow, at noon precisely, we will test one of these ideas."

⊙⟋⊙

The following day, an hour before noon, Sklar Hast rowed to the isolated pad on which Meth Cagno had established his workshop. Cagno himself was hard at work on an intricate contrivance whose purpose Sklar Hast could not fathom. A rectangular frame of stalk rose ten feet in the air, supporting a six-foot hoop of woven withe in a plane parallel to the surface of the float. To the hoop was glued a rather large sheet of pad-skin, which had been scraped, rubbed and oiled until it was almost transparent. Below Meth Cagno was arranging a box containing ashes. As Sklar Hast watched, he mixed in a quantity of water and some gum, enough to make a gray dough, which he worked with his fingers and knuckles, to leave a saucer-shaped depression.

The sun neared the zenith; Cagno signaled two of his helpers. One climbed up the staging; the other passed up buckets of water. The first poured these upon the transparent membrane, which sagged under the weight.

Sklar Hast watched silently, giving no voice to his perplexity. The membrane, now brimming, seemed to bulge perilously.

Meth Cagno, satisfied with his arrangements, joined Sklar Hast. "You are puzzled by this device; nevertheless it is very simple. You own a telescope?"

"I do. An adequately good instrument, though the gum is clouded."

"The purest and most highly refined gum discolors, and even with the most careful craftsmanship, lenses formed of gum yield distorted images, of poor magnification. On the Home World, according to Brunet, lenses are formed of a material called 'glass'."

The sun reached the zenith; Sklar Hast's attention was caught by a peculiar occurrence in the box of damp ash. A white-hot spot had appeared; the ash began to hiss and smoke. He drew near in wonderment. "Glass would seem to be a useful material," Meth Cagno was saying. "Brunet describes it as a mixture of substances occurring in ash together with a compound called 'silica' which is found in ash but also occurs in the husks of sea-ooze: 'plankton', so Brunet calls it. Here I have mixed ash and sea-ooze; I have constructed a water-lens to condense sunlight, I am trying to make glass..." He peered into the box, then lifted it a trifle, bringing the image of the sun to its sharpest focus. The ash glowed red, orange, yellow; suddenly it seemed to slump. With a rod Cagno pushed more ash into the center, until the wooden box gave off smoke, whereupon Cagno pulled it aside, and gazed anxiously at the molten matter in the center. "Something has happened; exactly what we will determine when the stuff is cool." He turned to his bench, brought forward another box, this half-full of powdered charcoal. In a center depression rested a cake of black-brown paste.

"And what do you have there?" asked Sklar Hast, already marveling at Cagno's ingenuity.

"Dried blood. I and my men have drained ourselves pale. Brunet reveals that blood contains iron. Now I will try to burn away the various unstable fluids and oozes, to discover what remains. I hope to find unyielding iron." Cagno thrust the box under the lens. The dried blood smouldered and smoked, then burst into a reeking flame which gave off a nauseous odor. Cagno squinted up at the sun. "The lens burns well only when the sun is overhead, so our time is necessarily limited."

"Rather than water, transparent gum might be used, which then would harden, and the sun could be followed across the sky."

"Unfortunately no gum is so clear as water," said Cagno regretfully. "Candle-plant sap is yellow. Bindlebane seep holds a blue fog."

"What if the two were mixed, so that the blue defeated the yellow? And then the two might be filtered and boiled. Or perhaps water can be coagulated with tincture of bone."

Cagno assented. "Possibly feasible, both."

They turned to watch the blood, now a glowing sponge which tumbled into cinders and then, apparently consumed, vanished upon the surface of the blazing charcoal. Cagno snatched the crucible out from under the lens. "Your blood seems not over-rich," Sklar Hast noted critically. "It might be wise to tap Barquan Blasdel and the other Intercessors; they appear a hearty lot."

Cagno clapped a cover upon the box. "We will know better when the charcoal goes black." He went to his bench, brought back another box. In powdered charcoal stood another tablet, this of black paste. "And what substance is this?" inquired Sklar Hast.

"This," said Meth Cagno, "is kragen blood, which we boiled last night. If man's blood carries iron, what will kragen blood yield? Now we discover." He thrust it under the lens. Like the human blood it began to smoulder and burn, discharging a smoke even more vile than before. Gradually the tablet flaked and tumbled to the surface of the charcoal; as before Cagno removed it and covered it with a lid. Going to his first box, he prodded among the cinders with a bit of sharp bone, scooped out a congealed puddle of fused material which he laid on the bench. "Glass. Beware. It is yet hot."

Sklar Hast, using two pieces of bone, lifted the object. "So this is glass. Hmm. It hardly seems suitable for use as a telescope lens. But it may well prove useful otherwise. It seems dense and hard—indeed, almost metallic."

Cagno shook his head in deprecation. "I had hoped for greater transparency. There are probably numerous impurities in the ash and sea-ooze. Perhaps they can be removed by washing the ash or treating it with acid, or something of the sort."

"But to produce acid, electricity is necessary, or so you tell me."

"I merely quote Brunet."

"And electricity is impossible?"

Cagno pursed his lips. "That we will see. I have hopes. One might well think it impossible to generate electricity using only ash, wood, water and sea-stuff—but we shall see. Brunet offers a hint or two. But first, as to our iron…"

The yield was small: a nodule of pitted gray metal half the size of a pea. "That bit represents three flasks of blood." Cagno remarked glumly. "If we bled every vein on the float we might win sufficient iron for a small pot."

"This is not intrinsically an unreasonable proposal," said Sklar Hast. "We can all afford a flask of blood, or two, or even more during the course of months. To think—we have produced metal entirely on our own resources!"

Cagno wryly inspected the iron nodule. "There is no problem to burning the blood under the lens. If every day ten of the folk come to be bled, eventually we will sink the pad under the accumulated weight of iron." He removed the lid from the third box. "But observe here! We have misused our curses! The kragen is by no means a creature to be despised!"

On the charcoal rested a small puddle of reddish-golden metal: three times as large as the iron nodule. "I presume this metal to be copper, or one of its alloys." said Cagno. "Brunet describes copper as a dark red metal, very useful for the purpose of conducting electricity."

Sklar Hast lifted the copper from the coals, tossed it back and forth till it was cool. "Metal everywhere! Nicklas Rile has been hacking apart the kragen for its bones. He is discarding the internal organs, which are black as snuff-flower. Perhaps they should also be burned under the lens."

"Convey them here, I will burn them. And then, after we burn the kragen's liver, or whatever the organ, we might attempt to burn snuff-flowers as well."

The kragen's internal organs yielded further copper. The snuff-flowers produced only a powder of whitish-yellow ash which Meth Cagno conscientiously stored in a tube labeled: ASH OF SNUFF-FLOWER.

ᏮᏏᎧ

Four days later the largest of the kragen seen so far reappeared. It came swimming in from the west, paralleling the line of floats. A pair of swindlers, returning to the float with a catch of gray-fish, were the first to spy the great black cylinder surmounted by its four-eyed turret. They bent to their oars, shouting the news ahead. A well-rehearsed plan now went into effect. A team of four young swindlers ran to a lightweight coracle, shoved off, paddled out to intercept the kragen. Behind the coracle trailed two ropes, each controlled by a gang of men. The kragen, lunging easily through the water, approached, swimming fifty yards off the float. The coracle eased forward, with one named Bade Beach going forward to stand on the gunwales. The kragen halted the motion of its vanes, to drift and eye the coracle and the derricks with flint-eyed suspicion.

The two swindlers yet at the oars eased the coracle closer. Bade Beach stood tensely, twitching a noose, while the fourth man controlled the lines to the float. The kragen, contemptuous of attack, issued a few nonplussed clicks of the mandibles, twitched the tips of its vanes, creating four whirlpools. The coracle eased closer, to within a hundred feet, eighty—sixty feet. Bade Beach bent forward. The kragen decided to punish the men for their provocative actions and thrust sharply forward. When it was but thirty feet distant, Bade Beach tossed a noose toward the turret—and missed. From the float came groans of disappointment. One of the gangs hastily jerked the coracle back. The kragen swerved, turned, made a second furious charge which brought it momentarily to within five feet of the coracle, whereupon Bade Beach dropped the noose over its turret. From the float came a cheer; both gangs hauled on their lines, one snatching the coracle back to safety, the other tightening the noose and pulling the kragen aside, almost as it touched the coracle.

Thrashing and jerking the kragen was dragged over to the sea-leaning derrick, and hoisted from the water in the same fashion as the first. This was a large beast: the derrick creaked, the float sagged; before the kragen heaved clear from the water sixty-five men were tugging on the end of the lift. The derrick tilted back, the kragen swung in over the float. The vanes were lashed, the beast lowered. Again the onlookers surged forward, laughing, shouting, but no longer exemplifying the fury with which they had attacked the first kragen.

At a distance a group of Intercessors watched with curled lips. They had not reconciled themselves to their new circumstances, and conscious of their status as the lowest of castes worked as little as possible. Chisels and mallets were plied against the kragen turret; the dome was pried loose, the nerve-nodes destroyed. Fiber buckets were brought, the body fluids were scooped out and carried off to evaporation trays.

Sklar Hast had watched from the side. This had been a large beast—about the size of King Kragen when first he had approached the Old Floats, a hundred and fifty years previously. Since they had successfully dealt with this creature, they need have small fear of any other—except King Kragen. And Sklar Hast was forced to admit that the answer was not yet known. No derrick could hoist King Kragen from the water. No line could restrain the thrust of his vanes. No float could bear his weight. Compared to King Kragen, this dead hulk now being hacked apart was a pygmy…From behind came a rush of feet; a woman tugged at his elbow, gasping and gulping in the effort to catch her breath. Sklar Hast, scanning the float in startlement, could see nothing to occasion her distress. Finally she was able to blurt: "Barquan Blasdel has taken to the sea, Barquan Blasdel is gone!"

"What!" cried Sklar Hast.

The woman told her story. For various reasons, including squeamishness and pregnancy, she had absented herself from the killing of the kragen, and kept to her hut at the far side of the float. Seated at her loom she observed a man loading bags into a coracle, but preoccupied with her own concerns she paid him little heed, and presently arose to the preparation of the evening meal. As she kneaded the pulp from which the bread-stuff known as pangolay was baked, It came to her that the man's actions had been noticeably furtive. Why had he not participated in the killing of the kragen? The man she had seen was Barquan Blasdel! The implications of the situation stunned her for a moment. Wiping her hands, she went to the hut where Blasdel and his spouse were quartered, to find no one at home. It was still possible that she was mistaken; Blasdel might even now be watching the killing of the kragen. So she hurried across the float to investigate. But on the way the conviction hardened:

the man indeed had been Barquan Blasdel, and she had sought out Sklar Hast with the information.

◎◎

From the first Barquan Blasdel had made no pretense of satisfaction with his altered circumstances. His former rank counted nothing, in fact aroused antagonism among his float-fellows. Barquan Blasdel grudgingly adapted himself to his new life, building sponge arbors and scraping withe. His spouse, who on Apprise Float had commanded a corps of four maidens and three garden-men, at first rebelled when Blasdel required her to bake pangolay and core sponges "like any low-caste slut", as she put it, but finally she surrendered to the protests of her empty stomach. Her daughters adopted themselves with bet-ter grace, and indeed the four youngest participated with great glee at the slaughter of the kragen. The remaining two stayed in the background, eyebrows raised disdainfully at the vulgar fervor of their sisters.

Barquan Blasdel, his spouse, his two older daughters and their lovers were missing, as was a sturdy six-man coracle to-gether with considerable stores. Sklar Hast despatched four coracles in pursuit, but evening had brought the west wind, and there was no way of determining whether Blasdel had paddled directly west, or had taken refuge in the jungle of floats at the western edge of the chain, where he could hide indefinitely.

The coracles returned to report no sign of the fugitives. The Council of Seven gathered to consider the situation. "Our mis-take was leniency," complained Robin Magram, a gnarled and weather-beaten old Swindler. "These Intercessors—Barquan Blasdel and all the rest—are our enemies. We should have made a complete job of it, and strangled them. Our qualms have cost us our security."

"Perhaps," said Sklar Hast. "But I for one cannot bring myself to commit murder—even if such murder is in our best interest."

"These other Intercessors now—" Magram jerked his thumb to a group of huts near the central pinion "—what of them? Each wishes us evil. Each is now planning the same despicable act as that undertaken by Barquan Blasdel and his spouse. I feel that they should be killed at once—quietly, without malice, but with finality."

His proposal met no great enthusiasm. Arrel Sincere, a Bezzler of complete conviction and perhaps the most caste-conscious man on the float, said glumly, "What good do we achieve? If Barquan Blasdel returns to the Old Floats, our refuge is known and we must expect inimical actions."

"Not necessarily," contended Meth Cagno. "The folk of the Old Floats gain nothing by attacking us."

Sklar Hast made a pessimistic dissent. "We have escaped King Kragen, we acknowledge no overlord. Misery brings jealousy and resentment. The Intercessors can whip them to a sullen fury." He pitched his voice in a nasal falsetto. "'Those insolent fugitives! How dare they scamp their responsibility to noble King Kragen? How dare they perform such bestial outrages against the lesser kragen? Everyone aboard the coracles! We go to punish the iconoclasts!'"

"Possibly correct," said Meth Cagno. "But the Intercessors

are by no means the most influential folk of the Floats. The Arbiters will hardly agree to any such schemes."

"In essence," said Phyral Berwick, "we have no information. We speculate in a void. In fact Barquan Blasdel may lose himself on the ocean and never return to the Old Floats. He may be greeted with apathy or with excitement. We talk without knowledge. It seems to me that we should take steps to inform ourselves as to the true state of affairs: in short, that we send spies to derive this information for us."

Phyral Berwick's proposal ultimately became the decision of the Seven. They also ordained that the remaining Intercessors be guarded more carefully, until it was definitely learned whether or not Barquan Blasdel had returned to the Old Floats. If such were the case the location of the New Floats was no longer a secret, and the consensus was that the remaining Intercessors should likewise be allowed to return, should they choose to do so. Nicklas Rile considered the decision soft-headed. "Do you think they would warrant us like treatment in a similar situation? Remember, they planned that King Kragen should waylay us!"

"True enough," said Arrel Sincere wearily, "but what of that? We can either kill them, hold them under guard, or let them go their ways, the last option being the least taxing and the most honorable."

Nicklas Rile made no further protest, and the council then concerned itself with the details of the projected spy operation. None of the coracles at hand were considered suitable, and it was decided to build a coracle of special design—long, light, low to the water, with two sails of fine weave to catch

every whisper of wind. Three men were named to the operation, all originally of Almack Float, a small community far to
the west, in fact next to·Sciona, the end of the chain. None
of the three men had acquaintance on Apprise and so stood
minimal chances of being recognized.

The coracle was built at once. A light keel of laminated and
glued withe was shaped around pegs; ribs were bent and lashed
into place; diagonal ribs were attached to these, then the whole
frame was covered with four layers of varnished pad-skin.

At mid-morning of the fourth day after Barquan Blasdel's
flight, the coracle, which was almost a canoe, departed to the
west, riding easily and swiftly over the sunny blue water. For
three hours it slid along the line of floats, each an islet be-
decked in blue, green and purple verdure, surmounted by the
arching fronds of prime plant, each surrounded by its constel-
lation of smaller pads. The coracle reached the final float of the
group and struck out west across the water. Water swirled and
sparkled behind the long oars, the men in their short-sleeved
white smocks working easily. Afternoon waned; the rain clouds
formed and came scudding with black brooms hanging below.
After the rain came sunset, making a glorious display among
the broken clouds. The breeze began to blow from the west;
the three men crouched and rowed with only sufficient force
to maintain headway. Then came the mauve dusk with the
constellations appearing and then night with the stars blazing
down on the glossy black water. The men took turns sleeping,
and the night passed. Before dawn the favoring wind rose; the
sails were set, the coracle bubbled ahead, with a chuckling of
bow-wave and wake. The second day was like the first. Just

before dawn of the third day the men lowered the horn into the water and listened.

Silence.

The men stood erect, looked into the west. Allowing for the increased speed of their passage, Tranque Float should be near at hand. But nothing could be seen but the blank horizons.

The dawn wind came; the sails were set, the coracle surged west. At noon the men, increasingly dubious, ceased paddling, and once more searched the horizons carefully. As before there was nothing visible save the line dividing dark blue from bright blue. The floats by now should be well within sight. Had they veered too far north or too far south?

The men deliberated, and decided that while their own course had generally been true west, the original direction of flight might have been something south of east: hence the floats in all probability lay behind the northern horizon. They agreed to paddle four hours to the north, then if nothing were seen, to return to the south.

Toward the waning of afternoon, with the rain-clouds piling up, far smudges showed themselves. Now they halted, lowered the horn, to hear crunch crunch crunch, with startling loudness. The men twisted the tube, to detect the direction of the sound. It issued from the north. Crouching low they listened, ready to paddle hastily away if the sound grew louder. But it seemed to lessen and the direction veered to the east. Presently it died to near inaudibility, and the men proceeded.

The floats took on substance, extending both east and west; soon the characteristic profiles could be discerned, and then the hoodwink towers. Dead ahead was Aumerge, with Apprise Float yet to the west.

So they paddled up the chain, the floats with familiar and beloved names drifting past, floats where their ancestors had lived and died: Aumerge, Quincunx, Fay, Hastings, Quatrefoil, with its curious cloverleaf configuration, and then the little outer group, the Bandings, and beyond, after a gap of a mile, Apprise Float.

The sun set, the hoodwink towers began to flicker, but the configurations could not be read. The men paddled the coracle toward Apprise. Verdure bulked up into the sky; the sounds and odors of the Old Floats wafted across the water, inflicting nostalgic pangs upon each of the men. They landed in a secluded little cove which had been described to them by Phyral Berwick, covered the coracle with leaves and rubbish. According to the plan, two remained by the coracle, while the third, one Henry Bastaff, moved across the float toward the central common and Apprise Market.

Hundreds of people were abroad on this pleasant evening, but Henry Bastaff thought their mood to be weary and even a trifle grim. He went to the ancient Apprise Inn, which claimed to be the oldest building of the floats: a long shed beamed with twisted old stalks, reputedly cut at the astounding depth of three hundred feet. Within was a long bar of laminated strips, golden-brown with wax and use; shelves behind displayed jars and tubes of arrack, beer, and spirits of life, while buffets to each end offered various delicacies and sweetmeats. To the front wide eaves thatched with garwort frond and lit by yellow and red lanterns protected several dozen tables and benches where travelers rested and lovers kept rendezvous. Henry Bastaff seated himself where he could watch both the Apprise hoodwink tower and that of Quatrefoil to the east. The serving maid approached; he ordered beer and nut-wafers. As he drank and ate he listened to conversations at nearby tables and read the messages which flickered up and down the line of floats.

The conversations were uninformative; the hoodwink messages were the usual compendium of announcements, messages, banter. Then suddenly in mid-message came a blaze, all eighteen lights together, to signal news of great importance. Henry Bastaff sat up straight on the bench.

"Important...information!...This...afternoon...Apprise... Intercessor...Barquan...Blasdel...kidnaped...by...the... rebels...returned...to...the...Floats...with...his...spouse...and... several...dependents....They...have...a...harrowing...tale...to... tell....The...rebels...are...established...on...a...float...to...the... east...where...they...kill...kragen...with...merciless...glee... and...plan...a...war...of...extermination...upon...the...folk... of...the...Old...Floats....Barquan...Blasdel...escaped...and... after...an...unnerving...voyage...across...the...uncharted... ocean...late...today...landed...on...Green...Lamp...Float.... He...has...called...for...an...immediate...convocation...to... consider...what...measures...to...take...against...the...rebels... who...daily...wax...in...arrogance."

CHAPTER V

FOUR DAYS LATER Henry Bastaff reported to the Seven. "Our arrival was precarious, for our initial direction took us many miles to the south of the Old Floats. Nevertheless we arrived. Apparently Blasdel experienced even worse difficulties for he reached Green Lamp Float about the same time that we landed on Apprise. I sat at the Old Tavern when the news came, and I saw great excitement. The people seemed more curious than vindictive, even somewhat wistful. A convocation was called for the following day. Since the folk of Almack Float would attend, I thought it best that Maible and Barway remain hidden. I stained my face, shaved eyebrows, mustache and hair, and at the convocation looked eye to eye with my Uncle Fodor the withe-peeler, who never gave a second glance.

"The convocation was vehement and lengthy. Barquan Blasdel resumed his rank of Apprise Intercessor. In my opinion

Vrink Smathe, who had succeeded to the post, found no joy in Blasdel's return.

"With great earnestness Blasdel called for a punitive expedition. He spoke of those who had departed as 'iconoclasts', 'monsters', 'vicious scum of the world, which it was the duty of all decent folk to expunge'.

"He aroused only lukewarm attention. No one showed heart for the project. The new Intercessors in particular were less than enthusiastic. Blasdel accused them of coveting their new posts, which they would lose if the old Intercessors returned. The new Intercessors refuted the argument with great dignity. 'Our concern is solely for the lives of men,' they said. 'What avail is there in destroying these folk? They are gone; good riddance. We shall maintain our ancient ways with more dedication because the dissidents have departed.'

"One of the new Intercessors had a crafty thought: 'Of course, if by some means we can direct King Kragen's attention to these fugitives, that is a different story.'

"Barquan Blasdel was forced to be content with this much. 'How can we do this?'

"'By our usual means for summoning King Kragen: how else?'

"Blasdel agreed. 'It is necessary to hurry. These evil folk kill kragen and smelt metal from the blood. They plan mischief against us, and we must rebuff them with decisive severity.'

"There was further discussion, but no clear resolutions, which exasperated Barquan Blasdel. The convocation dissolved; we caught the evening wind to the east."

The Seven considered Henry Bastaff's report. "At least we are in no immediate peril," ruminated Robin Magram. "It appears that our surest guarantee of security is our custody of the old Intercessors, who would supersede the new officials if rescued. So here is a powerful deterrent against any large-scale attack."

"Still, we always must fear discovery by King Kragen," stated Sklar Hast. "King Kragen is our basic enemy; it is King Kragen whom we must destroy."

After a minute's silence Arrel Sincere said, "That, at the moment, is in the nature of a remote day-dream. In the meantime we must prepare for various contingencies, including demolishment by King Kragen of our new facilities. Also we must maintain a continued source of information: in short, spies must presently return to the Old Floats."

Henry Bastaff looked uncomfortably at his mates. "I will volunteer, for at least one more trip. Much effort and delay could be avoided if it were possible to sail with more assurance of reaching the destination."

Meth Cagno said, "Brunet mentions the 'compass'—an iron needle which points always to the north. The iron is 'magnetized' by wrapping it in a coil of copper strands and passing an electric current through these strands. We have copper, we have iron."

"But no electricity."

"No electricity," agreed Meth Cagno.

"And no means of obtaining electricity."

"As to that—we shall see."

☉|☉

Four days later Meth Cagno summoned the Seven to his workshop. "You will now see electricity produced."

"What? In that device?" Sklar Hast inspected the clumsy apparatus. To one side a tube of hollow stalk five inches in diameter and twenty feet high was supported by a scaffold. The base was contained at one end of a long box holding what appeared to be wet ashes. The far end of the box was closed by a slab of compressed carbon, into which were threaded copper wires. At the opposite end, between the tube and wet ashes was another slab of compressed carbon.

"This is admittedly a crude device, unwieldy to operate and of no great efficiency," said Meth Cagno. "It does however meet our peculiar requirements: which is to say, it produces electricity without metal, through the agency of water pressure. Brunet describes it in his Dicta. He calls it the 'Rous machine'. The tube is filled with water, which is thereby forced through the mud, which is a mixture of ashes and sea-slime. The water carries an electric charge which it communicates to the porous carbon as it seeps through. By this means a small but steady and quite dependable source of electricity is at our hand. As you may have guessed, I have already tested the device, and so can speak with confidence." He turned, snapped his fingers, and his helpers mounted the scaffold carrying buckets of water which they poured into the tube. Meth Cagno connected the wires to a coil of several dozen revolutions. He brought forward a dish. On a cork rested a small rod of iron.

"I have already magnetized this iron," said Cagno. "Note how it points to the north? Now—I bring it near the end of the coil. See it jerk! Electricity is flowing in the wire!"

The other members of the Seven were impressed. "And this iron needle will now serve to guide Henry Bastaff?"

"So I believe. But the Rous machine provides an even more dramatic possibility. With electricity we can disassociate sea-water to produce, after certain operations, the acid of salt, and a caustic of countering properties as well. The acid can then be used to produce more highly concentrated streams of electricity—if we are able to secure more metal. There is iron in our blood: I ask myself, where does the iron originate? Which of our foods contains the iron? I plan to reduce each of our foods under the lens, as well as any other distinctive substance which might yield a concentration of metal." He turned, went to the table, returned with a glistening object. "Look. A bottle of glass. Bolin Hyse has produced this bottle. He fashioned a tube of copper, fixed it to a longer tube of withe, dipped the copper into molten glass and blew. The result—" Meth Cagno inspected the object critically "—is not beautiful. The glass is gray and streaked with ash. The shape is uncertain. Nevertheless—here is a glass bottle, produced from ash and sea-ooze. Eventually, we will be building devices of great intricacy."

"Subject to the indulgence of King Kragen," muttered Sklar Hast.

Meth Cagno threw up his hands. "King Kragen bah! We shall kill him. When next a kragen is brought to the derrick, allow me to deal with it. There are tests I wish to make."

CHAPTER vi

O N THE WORLD which had no name, there were no seasons, no variations of climate except those to be found by traversing the latitudes. Along the equatorial doldrums, where floats of sea-plant grew in chains and clots, each day was like every other, and the passage of a year could be detected only by watching the night sky. Though the folk had small need for accurate temporal distinctions, each day was numbered and each year named for some significant event. A duration of twenty-two years was a 'surge', and was also reckoned by number. Hence a given date might be known as the 349th day in the Year of Malvinon's Deep Dive during the Tenth Surge. Time-reckoning was almost exclusively the province of the Scriveners. To most of the folk life seemed as pellucid and effortless as the glassy blue sea at noon.

King Kragen's attack upon Tranque Float occurred toward

the year's end, which thereupon became the Year of Tranque's Abasement, and it was generally assumed that the following year would be known as the Year of the Dissenters' Going.

As the days passed and the year approached its midpoint, Barquan Blasdel, Apprise Intercessor, instead of allowing the memory of his kidnaping to grow dim, revived it daily with never-flagging virulence. Each evening saw a memorandum from Barquan Blasdel flicker up and down the chain of floats: "Vigilance is necessary. The dissidents are led by seven men of evil energy. They flout the majesty of King Kragen; they despise the folk who maintain old traditions and most especially the Intercessors. They must be punished and taught humility. Think well on this matter. Ask yourself how may the dissidents most expeditiously be chastened?"

The other Intercessors, while politely attending Blasdel's urgencies, did little to give them effect. Blasdel daily became more hectic. At a Conclave of Notables his demands that the floats assemble an armada to invade the new floats and destroy the dissidents was vetoed by the Arbiters, Guild Masters and Caste Chiefs, on the grounds of utter infeasibility and pointlessness. "Let them be," growled Emacho Feroxibus, Chief of the Quatrefoil Bezzlers. "So long as they do not molest us, why should we molest them? I for one don't care to risk drowning for so dismal a cause."

Barquan Blasdel, containing his temper, explained carefully, "The matter is more complex than this. Here is a group who have fled in order to avoid paying their due to King Kragen. If they are allowed to prosper, to make profit of their defection, then other folk may be tempted to wonder, why do we not do likewise? If the sin of kragen-killing becomes vulgar recreation, where is reverence? Where is continuity? Where is obedience to High Authority?"

"This may be true," stated Providence Dringle, Chief Hood-wink for the Populous Equity Float. "Nonetheless in my opinion the cure is worse than the complaint. And to risk a heretical opinion, I must say the benefits we derive from High Authority no longer seem commensurate with the price we pay."

Blasdel swung about in shock, as did the other Intercessors. "May I ask your meaning?" Blasdel inquired icily.

"I mean that King Kragen consumes six to seven bushels of choice sponges daily. He maintains his rule in the waters surrounding the floats, true, but what do we need fear from the lesser kragen? By your own testimony the dissidents have developed a method to kill the kragen with facility."

Blasdel said with frigid menace, "I can not overlook the fact that your remarks are identical to the preposterous ravings of the dissidents, who so rightly shall be obliterated."

"Do not rely on my help," said Providence Dringle.

"Nor mine," said Emacho Feroxibus.

The conclave had divided into two antagonistic camps, the Intercessors and certain others supporting Barquan Blasdel, though few favored the more extreme of his propositions.

From the foliage which surrounded the scene of the conclave came a crash and a muttered exclamation. A number of men sprang into the shrubbery. There was a confused scuffle, the sound of blows and exclamations, and presently a man was dragged out into the lamplight. His skin was dark, his face was bland and bare of hair.

Barquan Blasdel marched forward. "Who are you? Why do you lurk in these forbidden precincts?"

The man staggered and blinked foolishly. "Is this the tavern? Pour out the arrack, pour for all! I am a stranger on Apprise, I would know the quality of your food and drink."

Emacho Feroxibus snorted, "The fool is drunk, turn him off the float."

"No!" roared Blasdel, jerking forward in excitement. "This is a dissident, this is a spy! I know him well! He has shaved his head and his face, but never can he defeat my acuity! He is here to learn our secrets!"

The group turned their attention upon the man, who blinked even more vehemently. "A spy? Not I. I came to find the Old Tavern."

Blasdel sniffed the air in front of the captive's face. "There is no odor: neither beer nor arrack nor spirits of life. Come! All must satisfy themselves as to this so that there will be no subsequent contradictions and vacillations."

"What is your name?" demanded Vogel Womack, the Parnassus Arbiter. "Your float and your caste?"

The captive took a deep breath, cast off his pretense of drunkenness. "I am Henry Bastaff. I am a dissident. I am here to learn if you plan evil against us. That is my sole purpose."

"A spy!" cried Barquan Blasdel in a voice of horror. "A self-confessed spy!"

"It is a serious matter," said Emacho Feroxibus, "but the truth of the matter is undoubtedly as he has averred."

The Intercessors set up a chorus of indignant hoots and jibes. Barquan Blasdel said, "He is guilty of at least a double offense: first, the various illegalities entering into his dissidence; and second, his insolent attempt to conspire against us, the staunch and the faithful. The crime has occurred on Apprise Float, and affects our relations with King Kragen. Hence, I, Barquan Blasdel, am compelled to demand an extreme penalty. Parler Denk, the new Apprise Arbiter, in such instance, can implement such a penalty by simple executive command, without consultation with the council. Arbiter Denk, what is your response?"

"Be not hasty," warned Vogel Womack. "Tomorrow the man's deed will not appear so grave."

Barquan Blasdel ignored him. "Parler Denk, what is your response?"

"I agree, in all respects. The man is a vile dissident, an agent of turmoil and a spy. He must suffer an extreme penalty. To this declaration there will be allowed no appeal."

◌◌◌

On the following day a significant alteration was made in the method by which King Kragen was tendered his customary oblation. Previously, when King Kragen approached a lagoon with the obvious intent of feasting, arbors overgrown with sponges were floated to the edge of the net, for King Kragen to pluck with his palps. Now the sponges were plucked, heaped upon a great tray and floated forth between a pair of coracles. When the tray was in place, Barquan Blasdel went to his sanctum. King Kragen was close at hand; the scraping of his chitin armor sounded loud in Blasdel's listening device.

Blasdel sounded his submarine horn; the scraping ceased, then began once more, increasing in intensity. King Kragen was approaching.

He appeared from the east, turret and massive torso riding above the surface, the great rectangular swimming platform gliding through the ocean on easy strokes of his vanes.

The forward eyes noted the offering. King Kragen approached casually, inspected the tray, began to scoop the sponges into his maw with his forward palps.

From the float folk watched in somber speculation mingled with awe. Barquan Blasdel came gingerly forth to stand on the edge of the pad, to gesticulate in approval as King Kragen ate.

The tray was empty. King Kragen made no motion to depart; Blasdel swung about, gestured to an understudy. "The sponges: how many were offered?"

"Seven bushels. King Kragen usually eats no more."

"Today he seems to hunger. Are others plucked?"

"Those for the market: another five bushels."

"They had best be tendered King Kragen; it is not well to stint." While King Kragen floated motionless, the coracles were pulled to the float, another five bushels were poured upon the tray, and the tray thrust back toward King Kragen. Again he ate, consuming all but a bushel or two. Then, replete, he submerged till only his turret remained above the water. And there he remained, moving sluggishly a few feet forward, a few feet backward.

⊙⦶

Nine days later a haggard Denis Maible reported the capture of Henry Bastaff to the Seven. "On the following day King Kragen had not yet moved. It was clear that the new method of feeding had impressed him favorably. So at noon the tray was again filled, with at least ten bushels of sponge, and again King Kragen devoured the lot.

"During this time we learned that Henry Bastaff had been captured and condemned—indeed the news had gone out over the hoodwink towers—but we could not discover where he was imprisoned or what fate had been planned for him.

"On the third day Blasdel made an announcement, to the effect that the dissident spy had sinned against King Kragen and King Kragen had demanded the privilege of executing him.

"At noon the tray went out. At the very top was a wide board supporting a single great sponge; and below, the usual heap. King Kragen had not moved fifty yards for three days. He approached the tray, reached for the topmost sponge. It seemed fastened to the board. King Kragen jerked, and so decapitated Henry Bastaff, whose head had been stuffed into the sponge. It was a horrible sight, with the blood spouting upon the pile of sponges. King Kragen seemed to devour them with particular relish.

"With Henry Bastaff dead, we no longer had reason to delay—except for curiosity. King Kragen showed no signs of moving, of visiting the other floats. It was clear that he found the new feeding system to his liking. By then, Apprise Float was bereft of sponges.

"The Intercessors conferred by hoodwink and apparently arrived at a means of dealing with the situation. King Kragen's meal on the fourth day was furnished by Granolt Float and ferried to Apprise by coracle. On the fifth day the sponges were brought from Sankeston. It appears that King Kragen is now a permanent guest at Apprise Float…On the evening of the fifth day we launched our coracle and returned to New Float."

The Seven were silent. Phyral Berwick finally made a sound of nausea. "It is a repulsive situation. One which I would like to change."

Sklar Hast looked toward Meth Cagno. "There is the man who smelts metal."

Meth Cagno smiled wryly. "Our enterprises are multiplying. We have found a number of sources which when burnt in sufficiently large quantities produce at least four different metals. None seem to be iron. We have bled everyone on the float, twice or three times: this blood has yielded several pounds of iron, which we have hammered and refined until now it is hard and keen beyond all belief. Our electrical device has produced twenty-four flasks of acid of salt, which we maintain in bottles blown by our glass shop, which is now an establishment completely separated from the smelting."

"This is encouraging and interesting," said Robin Magram, "but what will it avail against King Kragen?"

Meth Cagno pursed his lips. "I have not yet completed my experiments, and I am unable to make an unequivocal answer. But in due course our preparations will be complete."

CHAPTER vii

SOME TWO HUNDRED days later, toward the end of the year, swindlers working the waters to the east of Tranque Float spied the armada from the east. There were two dozen canoes sheathed with a dull black membrane. Each canoe carried a crew of thirty, who wore helmets and corselets of the same black substance, and carried lances tipped with orange metal. They accompanied a strange craft, like none ever seen before along the floats. It was rectangular, and rode on four parallel pontoons. A bulwark of the black sheathing completely encircled the barge, to a height of five feet. Fore and aft rose stout platforms on which were mounted massive crossbow-like contrivances, the arms of which were laminated stalk and kragen chitin, and the string cables woven from strips of kragen leather. The hold of the barge contained two hundred glass vats, each of two quarts capacity, each two-thirds full of pale liquid. The barge was propelled by oars—a score on either side—and moved with not inconsiderable speed.

The swindlers paddled with all speed to Tranque Float and the hoodwink towers flickered an alarm: *"The...dissidents... are...returning...in...force!...They...come...in...strange... black...canoes...and...an...even...more...peculiar...black... barge....They...show...no...fear."*

The flotilla continued up the line of floats: Thrasneck, Bickle, Green Lamp, and at last Fay, Quatrefoil, and finally Apprise.

In the water before the lagoon lolled King Kragen—a bloat-ed monstrous King Kragen, dwarfing the entire flotilla.

King Kragen swung about, the monstrous vanes suck-ing whirlpools into the ocean. The eyes with opalescent films shifting back and forth within, fixed upon the black sheathing of canoe, barge and armor, and he seemed to recognize the substance as kragen hide, for he emitted a snort of terrible dis-pleasure, jerked his vanes, and the ocean sucked and swirled.

The barge swung sidewise to King Kragen. The two cross-bows, each cocked and strung, each armed with an iron har-poon smelted from human blood, were aimed.

King Kragen sensed menace. Why otherwise should men be so bold? He twitched his vanes, inched forward—to within a hundred feet. Then he lunged. Vanes dug the water; with an ear-shattering shriek King Kragen charged, mandibles snapping.

The men at the crossbows were pale as sea-foam; their fin-gers twitched. Sklar Hast turned to call, "Fire!" but his voice caught in his throat and what he intended for an incisive command sounded as a startled stammer. But the command was understood. The left crossbow thudded, snapped, sang: the harpoon, trailing a black cable sprang at King Kragen's turret, buried itself. King Kragen hissed.

The right crossbow fired; the second harpoon stabbed deep into the turret. Sklar Hast motioned with his hand to the men in the hold. "Connect." The men joined copper to copper. In the hold two hundred voltaic cells, each holding ten thin-leaved cathodes and ten thin-leaved anodes, connected first in four series of fifty, and these four series in parallel, poured a gush of electricity along the copper cables wrapped in varnished pad-skin, which led to the harpoons. Into King Kragen's turret poured the energy, and King Kragen went stiff. His vanes protruded at right angles to his body. Sklar Hast said to Meth Cagno, "Your experiments seem to be as valid as with the lesser kragen—luckily."

"I never doubted," said Meth Cagno.

Sklar Hast waved to the canoes. They swung toward King Kragen, beaching on the rigid subsurface platform. The men swarmed up the torso. With mallets and copper chisels they attacked the lining between dome and turret wall. There was thirty feet of seam, but many hands at work. The lining was broken; bars were inserted into the crack; all heaved. With a splitting sound the dome was dislodged. It slid over and into the water; the men leapt down into the knotted gray cords and nodes and began hacking.

On Apprise Float a great throng had gathered. One man, running back and forth, was Barquan Blasdel. Finally he persuaded several score of men to embark in coracles and attack the flotilla. Eight black canoes were on guard. Paddles dug the water, the canoes picked up momentum, crashed into the foremost coracles, crushing the fragile shells, throwing the men into the water. The canoes backed away, turned toward the other coracles, which retreated.

Out in the lagoon King Kragen's nerve nodes had been cast into the sea. The harpoons were extracted, the flow of electricity extinguished.

King Kragen floated limp, a lifeless hulk. The men plunged into the sea to wash themselves, clambered back up on the dead swimming platform, boarded their canoes.

The barge now eased toward Apprise Float. Barquan Blasdel gesticulated to the folk like a crazy man. "To arms! Stakes, chisels, mallets, knives, bludgeons! Smite the miscreants!"

Sklar Hast called to the throng, "King Kragen is dead. What do you say to this?"

There was silence; then a faint cheer and a louder cheer, and finally uproarious celebration.

Sklar Hast pointed a finger at Barquan Blasdel. "That man must die. He murdered Henry Bastaff. He has fed your food to the vile King Kragen. He would have continued doing so until King Kragen over-grew the entire float."

Barquan Blasdel made the mistake of turning to flee—an act which triggered the counter-impulse to halt him. When he was touched, he smote, and again he erred, for the blow brought a counter-blow and Barquan Blasdel was presently torn to pieces.

"What now?" called the crowd. "What now, Sklar Hast?"

"Nothing whatever, unless you choose to kill the other Intercessors. King Kragen is dethroned; our duty is done. We now return to the New Floats."

From the shore someone called out, "Come ashore, men of the New Floats, and share our great joy. Greet your old friends, who long have been saddened at your absence! Tonight the arrack will flow and we will play the pipes and dance in the light of our yellow lamps!"

Sklar Hast shook his head, waved his hand and called back: "Now we return to the New Floats. In a week certain of us will return, and the weeks after that will see constant traffic between Old and New Floats, and out to floats still unknown. King Kragen is dead, the lesser kragen are our prey, so who is there to stop us? Now that we know metal and glass and electricity, all things are possible. Rejoice with all our good will. For now, farewell."

The barge and the canoes swung about; oars and paddles dipped into the ocean, the black flotilla receded into the east, and disappeared.